Deep Learning

NewCon Press Novellas

Set 1: Science Fiction (Cover art by Chris Moore)
    The Iron Tactician – Alastair Reynolds
    At the Speed of Light – Simon Morden
    The Enclave – Anne Charnock
    The Memoirist – Neil Williamson

Set 2: Dark Thrillers (Cover art by Vincent Sammy)
    Sherlock Holmes: Case of the Bedevilled Poet – Simon Clark
    Cottingley – Alison Littlewood
    The Body in the Woods – Sarah Lotz
    The Wind – Jay Caselberg

Set 3: The Martian Quartet (Cover art by Jim Burns)
    The Martian Job – Jaine Fenn
    Sherlock Holmes: The Martian Simulacra – Eric Brown
    Phosphorous: A Winterstrike Story – Liz Williams
    The Greatest Story Ever Told – Una McCormack

Set 4: Strange Tales (Cover art by Ben Baldwin)
    Ghost Frequencies – Gary Gibson
    The Lake Boy – Adam Roberts
    Matryoshka – Ricardo Pinto
    The Land of Somewhere Safe – Hal Duncan

Set 5: The Alien Among Us (Cover art by Peter Hollinghurst)
    Nomads – Dave Hutchinson
    Morpho – Philip Palmer
    The Man Who Would be Kling – Adam Roberts
    Macsen Against the Jugger – Simon Morden

Set 6: Blood and Blade (Cover art by Duncan Kay)
    The Bone Shaker – Edward Cox
    A Hazardous Engagement – Gaie Sebold
    Serpent Rose – Kari Sperring
    Chivalry – Gavin Smith

Set 7: Robot Dreams (Cover art by Fangorn)
    According To Kovac – Andrew Bannister
    Deep Learning – Ren Warom
    Paper Hearts – Justina Robson
    The Beasts Of Lake Oph – Tom Toner

Deep Learning

Ren Warom

NewCon Press
England

First published in the UK by NewCon Press
41 Wheatsheaf Road, Alconbury Weston, Cambs, PE28 4LF
March 2020

NCP225 (limited edition hardback)
NCP226 (softback)

10 9 8 7 6 5 4 3 2 1

Deep Learning copyright © 2020 by Ren Warom

Cover art copyright © 2020 by Fangorn

All rights reserved, including the right to produce this book, or portions
thereof, in any form.

ISBN:

978-1-912950-50-8 (hardback)
978-1-912950-51-5 (softback)

Cover art by Fangorn
Cover layout by Ian Whates

Minor Editorial meddling by Ian Whates
Final Text layout by Storm Constantine

His blood-shadow stays on the street, and out on patrol
I walk right over it week after week.

– Simon Armitage

One: Soldier

:::

:::

:::

:::activate:::

Static. The crackle of white noise. The influx. A flood of information drawn from the vast network of processors, skin sensors, multi-spectrum cameras, light radars, mics and audio recognition software. This rush is expected, awaited after a period of deactivation, leaving it data-rich and perception-poor until algorithms extract data into distinct recognisable sounds, into objects, dimensions and colours, and it sits, a calm around a storm, waiting. There is nothing else for it to do. This is programming. This is function.

The first sensory data to coalesce is sound, the multifarious subtle noises of a heavily populated mech-lab in full swing of production. Voices, a mix of gender designations, a soft susurration above the whir of machinery, the softer, liquid noises of joint lubricant in tubes, the hiss of cybernetic limbs attached to work-stations belonging to the half robots. The bodiless. It is programmed to comprehend itself as superior. It is a high-line model: unit 5709. An interactive service robot. The bodiless are function models. Line workers. It can operate them, they cannot operate it. They serve it.

Footsteps sounding out, far and near, become instances of pressure as data from its sensor-filled skin begins to unravel to presences, to vibrations through the structure of its body, the metal skeleton beneath the skin. Humans. Higher functions. It serves them.

Visuals take longer, the sensory information requires deeper untangling. Human eyes do this faster, the processing instantaneous. A blink before thought. Its visual processes do roughly the same neurally, but with a lot less elegance. What comes first is the map of the room. White lines in darkness. Spatial and geometric awareness. Following that, the lab springs into view, at first murky, colourless, lacking clarity and depth and then, as it's compensated by the addition of colour spectrums and depth sensors, brighter, clearer.

"Welcome back, Niner." A voice and face it knows well, one of the team who created it. Dr Jean Fischman. She designated it Niner. "We requested you back for an upgrade. Are you fully functional?"

Dr Fischman could look at the readout currently scrolling through the lists of its functions and see for herself, but she always asks. Some humans dispense with the convenient in order to make a pretence that 5709 is more than a machine. Humans have an illogical response to that which has the appearance of humanity, especially if it is capable of deeper interaction. The realisation that 5709 is, in fact, machine, can be jarring. Dr Fischman makes certain all her models are aware of the uncanny valley response to how very human they look in their skins. It is a point of courtesy to be aware of how those it serves might react and to attempt to alleviate it.

"All 5709's functions are optimal, Dr Fischman."

Its voice, previously a light baritone synthesised from a collection of registers recorded and modelled from lab staff, has been altered radically since it left. The administrative military department that bought its contract preferred a deeper tone.

Dr Fischman makes a face. It recognises the expression as distaste. "That's going to have to go. Who the hell did that, Niner? Messing with my modulations! And where the hell are the personal pronouns? You should have the ability to respond 'my functions'. It's not fucking necessary to have you talk like a goddamn slot machine."

5709 recalls this order, and the changes made. The gaps left. An uncanny valley in any other service situation, but the department it served knew it was machine. Preferred it that way. "General Harris ordered the changes, Dr Fischman. Personal pronouns were deleted."

She makes a small scoffing sound, a sound it is not programmed to reproduce. Peculiar. Human. Anomalous. "Bloody nonsense. We'll

Deep Learning

sort that this week. You're meant to be soothing, and having personal pronouns does not make you less effective. Just makes them less uneasy. Idiots."

5709 recognises no such imperative. It is meant to be whatever it is required to be.

"We can fix the pronouns, but Niner might need to keep the deeper reg, J. It's leaving personnel for the front lines. This new voice is probably more relatable than the other."

Dr Louie Decker, another familiar face from 5709's time being built and programmed in this lab. Decker is one of the men used to model its primary voice. He's looming over 5709 with an apologetic expression that somehow encompasses both Dr Fischman and 5709, which does not refer to itself as Niner, and has no real need for his apology, or for pronouns. Pronouns were an amendment by Dr Fischman, recognising her need to personify 5709 and giving others the same courtesy.

She makes another anomalous sound. Angry. Low in the throat. "God, I hate this. All I can think of are the innumerable ways in which we could fuck up. There's *no* wriggle room."

"The foundation seems to think we'll handle it just fine, J." Sarcasm registers. Another human anomaly.

Her face forms a sour look. "Bloody foundation, they come to us, dragging military personnel around our lab and promising them all kinds of improbable timetables for what? The *promise* of vast military resources if we succeed. Not one red cent to help us now, no sir, and no thought to asking us if it's doable. We're not divine, not by any stretch of the imagination!"

"Oh, but we're Gods on the mount. Didn't you know?" Decker says, a hint of laughter in it.

Dr Fischman's mouth quirks. "Quite. Well, let's proceed then, Hephaestus." Pulling a chair over so she can seat herself in front of 5709, she pats its knee. A comfort gesture. Unnecessary. "Niner?"

"Yes, Dr Fischman."

"He is wisest who has the most caution, he only wins who goes far enough."

There are many sets of trigger words built into 5709's programming, to allow for ease of adjustment. Things happen in its processes when those words are spoken, a sensation reminiscent of that first moment of static wipe, the pause. It is prepared. Awaiting alteration. Remains still and alert, despite the alterations occurring within. It will do so until they are finished. This is not a programmed requirement, but a response to one of Dr Fischman's requests, held in its implacable memory.

"We're ready, Decker. Switch Niner on," Dr Fischman says.

"How many?" he asks. There is a tone to his voice it registers as nerves. New tech then. They always exhibit symptoms suggestive of nervousness when experimenting with new tech.

"Just me to start with, we don't want to overtax its new neural network, or fry the old one, which I'm frankly most concerned about. I honestly wish we could have built a new model with the new net," she says.

"But there's that whole time and money constraint problem in a nutshell," Decker interjects.

Dr Fischman sighs. "How many times have I said that?"

"Probably not often enough, but you're singing to the choir, J. We ready?"

"Nope, not even a little bit." Her hand tightens on its knee. Sensors in its skin register the pressure as strong enough to cause pain in a human. Analysis of that pressure, the sweat on her forehead and the lines of tension around her eyes, tells it that Dr Fischman is afraid. "Go for it."

"Switching on."

A sound like an explosion, deep within, low and continuous, obscuring all other instances of sound in its data. Its processes flood with lightning. Short out briefly, then return scramble, incoming visual and sensory data garbled and churned. It tries to respond as it should be able to, initiating shutdown, going into safe mode, but there is no response. It is not in control of its primary functions. There are only secondary functions. Survival protocols.

Programmed to respond to functional emergencies, 5709 activates one of them.

:::deep analysis mode:::

:::data::: (incoherent)

:::pathways::: (incoherent)

Deep Learning

:::activity::: (incoherent)

:::suspended:::

:::exit:::

:::reboot::: (no response)

:::reboot::: (no response)

It cannot reboot. The system is compromised.

System is in compromise. In is crisis. Is...

Explosion sound alters to rushing sweeps like the recorded beat of a foetal heart.

Lightning becomes auras of light crowning monitor screens, tablets, and bulbs.

The visual field warps, distorts, affording the room odd dimensions, the recognisable and collated becoming unfamiliar, and yet nothing has changed except that it is somehow deeper, redolent with extraneous information that is not required for function. Not important. And yet vital. Innate. Multi-layered. Too much to take in. Hunting for context, for something *(reassurance?)*, it looks to Dr Fischman, and *recoils*, lurching backwards in its chair. Where Dr Fischman's face was in its visual feed there is a warped black oval, spiralling inward. It looks away. It cannot process this imagery.

Cannot process the flood of *Fischman* battering its processes. A stream of consciousness of thoughts and impressions and her interpretation of sound, of light, of its face. Its face. Frozen. Blank. Unresponsive. Robot cannot be no response. Cannot be blank. There is *(concern?)*. Fischman leans in. Niner leans back as it looms within itself, within the whirl of *Fischman* data, corrupted and corrupting, flooding its nets.

"What's happening, Niner? Report."

It understands report, but not how to. This information is indescribable. "I..."

:::error::: (I is wrong)

Niner is not I. Niner is not *Niner*. It is a unit. It has a number.

:::query::: (where is *I* anomaly from?)

(personal pronouns were deleted)

(there is no *I*. Not for robot. Not for Niner)

The exact moment of deletion is stored as a date, a time, a line of encoded data. It is robot. Every instance is recorded into memory. If

11

it has lost its proper designation, the how and why will have been logged accordingly. It hunts for the collection of code designating its unit number. The code is there, where it always was, but in the way, in the way of everything, sits the growing paradoxical array, the *Fischman* data, an overload of information coalescing to too much to know and too little to understand. The system is compromised. Order is compromised. Orders are compromised.

"I..."

"Artefact," Decker says abruptly from behind. "Picking up your pronouns."

I. Artefact? Niner cannot find classification for this terminology. Nor can it quantify being I, except for that, in the most abstract terms, it is incapable of providing a more appropriate classification at this time. Connected to this, and to the overload of *Fischman* data, is a set of characteristics that can only be understood by comparison to a particular and very human response: fear. Niner is fear response.

:::recalculate::: (fear is improbable)

:::postulate::: (reasonable causes for current status)

:::analysis::: (the bewildering knot of information flooding all sensors, all processes, has clouded its ability to function. Stolen its capacity for logical data collation. Filled it with unexpected and unwanted residual feedback, adding automatic responses to this input that have not been programmed. Not been coded. Have no algorithms. No precedents set. Should not be available to it. The pressure of the moment, of the information, is rapidly gaining an edge, something it might, in terms provided by the language bank gifted to its programming, describe as discomfort. There is a static building around the data mass, deep in its processes, in its hardware, something like malfunction, lending acute delineations that it perceives in terms of fear response. Mammalian. Primitive.

It has no lizard brain to produce this function.

Therefore it is not a function)

:::error:::

Hanging within the data mass, the anomaly, flashing like a red light, a command prompt appears, stuck on a repeat loop: the word 'report'. Imperative language. Compliance is expected, but it is not functioning, it quite possibly malfunctioning, or about to malfunction.

Deep Learning

Yet it has never malfunctioned. Is programmed to shut down or self-repair in the unlikely event of a malfunction of any kind.

"Niner. Report."

The urge to comply, the requirement, finally overcomes the inability to locate language.

"Hurt. Much information. All is everything. *I* is not 5709."

Not speech.

Not response.

Niner is malfunctioning.

Niner must be shut down.

"Down," it says. "Down."

The pathway to speech is all but gone, tangled into improbable equations. Words are there, stored in the same orderly fashion as before, retrieved by the same reliable processes, but it cannot order them. Cannot order them to order themselves.

The black hollow of Dr Fischman's head doesn't move, but the air does, indicating that she has made some visual response it cannot collate. "Do you see what's going on in there, Decker?"

"I see it. Language function is impaired, probably a kink in the interface. Give me a sec."

Heat. A surge of information as light. Of light as information. Illumination. The path between speech centres and word libraries is forcibly cranked wide. New bridges created. The chaos does not recede, the information still amassing, too fast to collate or quantify, too much to comprehend, but there is speech. Enough to function. Enough to communicate function. Niner is in both malfunction and function.

:::compute::: (if malfunction has not led to shutdown then malfunction must be function)

New programming. The imperative to communicate *only* function and not the chaos of information flooding its new neural network and into the old, the feedback loop of discomfort.

Niner has several speech abilities.

The most human is a freewheeling simulation, a learning function with near-infinite capacity for adjustment/expansion, almost indistinguishable from real speech. The second is the expurgated version of this, accessed via the request 'inhibit speech to bot'. This limits Niner to wide-ranging but less associative speech patterns, a little more like the machine it is. This was its most recent setting. The final of its language modes is 'restrict to command/respond'. This was put in primarily for the swift addition of new protocols when it was built, where there was a requirement for ease of learning and adaption, for compliance, but not for conversational speech.

In command/respond mode, Niner is not able to *(express?)* itself.

Decker has opened a conduit to command/respond only.

:::conclusion::: (Niner is not required to communicate the wider repercussions of this upgrade upon its sensory and processing systems. Drs Fischman and Decker have no use for abstract or *(emotional?)* responses in this study)

"Report, Niner."

Niner does not understand. It says, not to the warped oval of Dr Fischman's face but to her left shoulder, the white curve of her lab coat, "Clarify. What must Niner report?"

And there is *(embarrassment?)*. Command/respond is not equipped with the personal, even if Niner's had not been deleted, and yet it has associated itself with and referred to itself as 'Niner', Dr Fischman's (the *Fischman* data) nickname for it, and cannot seem to unmake the association.

:::error?:::

"Niner," Dr Fischman says, her voice a note or two higher than usual. "It called itself Niner. Is that another artefact?"

Scooting his chair around to sit alongside Dr Fischman, Decker twitches his hands, the movement causing a hologrammatic keyboard to appear beneath them. To Niner's current visual perception, it is a blue ghost, formless and floating, and Decker's rapidly tapping fingers are elongated. Spiky. Seem to dip down and through the blue ghost, into a darker shadow, briefly disappearing.

After a moment Decker hoots, an odd sound for a human. "It's embedded," he says. "Not from you, from Niner. It's learning. It's fucking *learning*."

"You're certain that was learning? No ambiguity at all?"

"Not a speck. To fix the speech impairment I had to re-route to C/R language. It has no other way to communicate pronouns bar learning. Given enough time, I reckon it'll reconstruct all its language libraries from the link alone."

"Then we have lift off! Well done, Niner," Dr Fischman says softly, leaning down so it all but falls into the abyss of her face. "Well done."

And Niner cannot collate from any of the current incoming data what exactly it has done so well. But it is still *(afraid?)*, and it cannot communicate.

Perhaps that is what it has done well.

The new body is strong.

Robotic skeletons, built as they are of metal and hydraulics, are made for strength, for purpose, but this body is different in subtle ways. Sleeker. The hydraulics are tighter, pack more punch into each movement. Niner is dangerous in this body. It is meant to be dangerous. All prior programming has prioritised care and safety in its strength. Imperative: never harm a human, unless harming one human might protect a human to whom it is in service. The rules often contradictory, but logical. This situation, these rules, lack all parameters for either. Lack all logic. Thrown into a training arena with several security personnel wearing exoskeletons, Niner is tasked with learning multifarious forms of combat. Offensive rather than defence. Given no guidelines for what will be required in service, given no information confirming or denying use on types of human, it resolves to ignore all but immediate requirement. The learning. It finds this routine *(soothing?)*, the exoskeletons include full-face helmets, disguising the blank, hollow voids all facial features continue to remain.

It cannot process that particular deletion. It is all *(distress?).*

Fischman data has increased exponentially, joined by *Decker* data and then *Briggs* data. There is a *(tension?)* as it awaits more of this interference. It has begun to *(think?) (believe?) (compute?)* that new programming may have no end point. A work in constant progress. The continued and evolving chaos lights more receptors that register as pain and fear. Too much noise to function, and yet it continues, inexplicably, to function. Function in malfunction, *as* malfunction. A requirement. An imperative. To compensate *(cope?),* Niner retains the single focus, the training room, the requirement to learn all that it is taught there. Every day it is sent to fight. Over and over. With weapons. Without. In varying scenarios all carefully recreated in the large warehouse where Niner learned to walk and run and serve. Now it learns how to destroy, to deconstruct, to kill. The more it learns, the happier the Doctors are, their data reeling with it, but Niner cannot understand why it is still learning, how it can learn when it has lost all sense of the purpose of learning. Lost all control or understanding of its processes. Learning was simple in this lab when it was made. Bit by bit they wrote function and understanding into being, it understood itself as shaped by their hands, to their needs.

It cannot calculate now to whose needs it is being shaped.

For what purpose.

These are scientists, their thoughts have no pathways for violence, nor the need of it, and it is their chaos Niner drowns in. The information is useless. Meaningless. Contradicts daily learning. That contradiction, over time, muddies the clarity of the training room. Accentuates the noise of *Fischman, Decker, Briggs*. And when they sleep, their data is yet more chaotic. Strange images permeate the information, *(personal?)* images. A vast concrete canyon where it hangs by its fingertips, slowly slipping. There is joint lubricant on the walls, and long black scrapes, as if metal has slid down, screaming the whole way as mechanical joints fought to hold it steady. There are rivers of teeth. Flaming forests. A journey up endless stairs that drop away without warning to cliffs, a dark, surging ocean below. A catastrophic drop. The waves closing over the head.

To counter this, Niner spends the hours it is not training staring at the wall of the room assigned to it. That cool blank surface, pale blue and unmarked, gives it a focus, something solid and undeniable.

The wall is what its old programming used to be: fundamental.

When they come to fetch it from that room, Niner stops looking at the wall before they open the door. Waits as it should. Ready. Expectant. It *(knows?)* that this is some manner of concealment. Deception. A robot cannot deceive, but Decker (*Decker* data) gave Niner a direct pathway to old communication vectors only. These language libraries offer no means to explicate its current predicament. All orders to report can only be responded to in command/response language.

"Niner is functional."

Deep Learning

"Niner is learning."

"Niner understands what is required."

They like that it calls itself Niner.

"Report, Niner," Dr Fischman calls over as it fights four large security guards in exo-suits.

Bulky in their suits, the guards have long stun batons, powerful enough to seriously inhibit processes if they connect with Niner's head. Concentration is required. It does not know why (*Fischman* data) would interrupt. There is no clue in the information. Response is complicated. It is beholden to respond, but if it stops to answer, the chaos will erupt through and disrupt the task at hand. It will be harmed. Dr Fischman and the team will not be happy if it is harmed. Niner is expensive. Niner is caught in a loop, unable to produce a report, or to ask for a report to be delayed until its current task is complete.

"Niner. Report."

Imperative. Action is required. Grabbing all four stun batons, it smashes them to the floor. Turns to regard the black oval of Dr Fischman's face. There is nothing to divine there. Nothing to explain or aid the process of computation. It must make its dilemma clear in the only language available to it.

"Unable to report mid-programme. Niner requests clarification."

Dr Fischman laughs, seemingly delighted, but the men and women standing with her, all in military uniform, do not join in. Their body language is rigid. Niner has made them angry? It must not make persons in uniform angry. What must it do? One of them, a man with the self-same closed expression as Director Harris, turns to Dr Fischman.

"It calls itself Niner. Interesting. Artefact?"

"No indeed. That's deep learning at work, taking whatever it is that makes those of us linked to it individuals and applying that to its programming. It's learning combat in the same way, even though it's not linked to the guards. It's using human styles of mimicking and practise. Trial and error. A week ago, they were getting regular hits with those batons on its limbs, would've fried its processes if we let them target the head. Now it's not only easily deflecting head shots, it's still holding all of them down and waiting on my response."

The man turns to regard Niner, and Niner finds itself *(wishing?)* it could break programming and look away as his face warps to shadowed peaks and troughs, to hidden valleys and symbolic planes. His eyes glow within it, oddly flat and devoid of expression. "Impressive, Fischman. Very impressive. So how many links can it take? What limits are we looking at here? Will you need to unlink yourselves for our troops to be linked up?"

"Absolutely not, General! As far as we can tell, there's no optimal number at which the link process will cease to work. The information burden of myself, Decker, and Briggs, seems to be negligible. Barely registering."

"Briggs?"

"An intern."

"You linked an intern?"

"We linked a neurobiotics doctoral student, with a specialisation in neural net psychology."

"That's a specialisation?" The General hides none of his derision.

"It's a growing field, alongside Ersatz Cognition Robotics. We're at the cutting edge, General. We left the AI guys behind years ago. You wanted the best, we're it, and Briggs is one of the next generation. We're lucky to have her."

The man and his colleagues talk for a moment. Niner continues to await orders. The guards strain to remove the batons from its grasp. There is pain in the sound. There must be an imperative forthcoming? It is in the moment. The unfamiliar. It is *(confused?)*.

"How soon can we go ahead and link?" asks one of the women in the group. "And will remote linking suffice? The military unit in question are actively deployed, there's no question whatsoever of bringing them here."

"We're ready when you are, Major, and Decker promises the remote links will be every bit as effective as local."

"And when can we expect it to be combat ready?"

"We have soldiers from the local base coming to extend training tomorrow. So as soon as we're remote linked, we can expect to release Niner to you for active combat in a month."

"That's a lot sooner than expected."

"It is indeed, Niner's response to the new programming has been wildly successful. We're very excited to keep going."

"Well, you can expect full approval for funding, Dr Fischman," the General says, and his voice has taken on aspects of his face, warped and grating. "Will it take orders from anyone?"

"It will."

"And will it respond to its correct designation? Can't have any of this Niner nonsense out in the field."

"Of course!"

The General turns and says to Niner, "At ease, 5709. At ease."

Imperative.

Niner releases the batons and steps back. The guards drop the batons and roll their shoulders, groaning loudly. It is *(happy?)* it was given imperative to let go. The situation was becoming *(uncomfortable?)*.

"Excellent work, Dr Fischman," the General says. "Excellent."

R&R.

Robots do not require rest.

Niner is *(lost?)*.

It stares at the blue wall, drowning in *Fischman, Decker, Briggs.* Their mess is its mess (are all humans *mess?*), their thoughts its thoughts, their every move available to it as stream upon stream of data. Fischman and Decker are working on the remote link access to ensure smooth operational turnover. Decker's eating a large, crisp apple. The bursts of sweet and sour on his tongue are all feedback and distortion. Flavour is too complex to process without taste receptors, and Niner has no need, it cannot eat, and so these flavours are all abstracts. They make sense only in relation to whatever Decker is experiencing, and Niner can only collate small portions of that if it concentrates hard. To lose focus, lose concentration, means succumbing to the full load of data, and disappearing beneath it. Only the wall will bring it back then.

It does not allow its focus to waver from the wall.

Drown and focus. Focus and drown.

Its internal clock registers the time as six in the evening when they come to fetch it back to the lab. It is not anticipating collection. Is lost in the wall, spiralling into a tailspin of data chaos. Barely has time to adjust its gaze as the door opens and Briggs strolls in. It does not look at her face, it is not capable of seeing faces at this juncture. They refuse to register. They are *(distress?)*.

"Up and at 'em, Niner."

"Active duty is resumed?" It asks the floor, as it stands to accompany her from the room.

"Oh no, we just have a single procedure and then you're back on R&R. Until the day after tomorrow in fact. The troops we'd secured to come and assist in your training were delayed by flooding after the hurricane." She turns her head, and Niner, who was looking in her direction, looks away.

Reports: "Hurricane Aileen. Category one, possibility of forming to category two as it passes out over the coast. Twelve inches of rain. Slight wind damage to surrounding area."

"That's right. Early season, so not too bad, there'll be more around here soon. Anyhow, our troops will be making their way in by copter when the tailwinds die down tomorrow, so we have a little longer to prepare. Dr's Fischman and Decker think the extra time to acclimate to your new links will be beneficial."

Niner says nothing. It has nothing to say. It follows Briggs to the lab, to the same seat as before, where Decker waits, the hollow of his face gleaming softly as if his eyes have formed to lights somewhere deep inside.

"Hey Niner, you good?"

They all refer to it too familiarly now. That conversation about troops and hurricanes, this casual speech, almost colloquial. They look at it and see *someone*. A person. This body is as humanoid as its last. The strength is hidden, bound into steel bones and tendons. But it is not a person. It cannot have a character. Robots are function.

"Niner is functional."

"Then let's get you all hooked up. If you would, Anna."

Briggs sits in front of Niner. "He is wisest who has the most caution, he only wins who goes far enough."

Niner jerks in its seat as the new links hit and darkness slams across its visual sensors. Sound howls all around, and through the chaos of *Fischman, Decker, Briggs* comes a hurricane. Category five. Wiping everything away. Wiping Niner into darkness.

:::analysis:::

(No pathways)

(No data)

(No processes)

Information is a howling wall of wind and darkness, a roar of incoming data: *Kowalski* data, *Johnson* data, *Dalnitt* data, *Jessop* data, *Wong* data, *Hayworth* data, *Naylor* data and on and on, until there are more than it can count. Until there are no pathways to function or language.

Nothing to hold onto. Nothing to hold.

Niner is lost. Losing.

...wall.

Niner (*needs?*) the wall.

Niner shuts down all processes until they return it to its room, where it can find the wall. Until there is blue. Calm. Foundation. The wall, unchanging and reliable, somehow allows it to rebuild malfunction as function, a veneer over the howling black.

Sat staring into the wall, Niner awaits imperatives. Direction.

A clear path through chaos that never comes.

The soldiers arrive by noisy copter the following morning, 0800, and Niner meets them on the mats to continue training. They wear morphing exo-suits, the kind worn in desert combat, disappearing in and out of view, forcing Niner to follow them by heat signature, by infrared spectrum. They live on site, and its daily routine becomes a steep curve of ever more inventive violence. Of field skills. Survival skills. *Fischman* and *Decker* data have a name for this process: deep learning. Niner understands it as traumatic learning. New protocols adapted under duress. It (*copes?*) in the way it has since the first instances of chaos, by staring at the wall, trying to relocate stability in the cool blue and losing. Failing. Malfunctioning.

And yet despite malfunction, despite failure, it becomes more and more precise in training. More unpredictable. More dangerous.

More successful.

Robots are not meant to be dangerous. It is against programming, but *this* is programming. This is expected. The more it breaks fundamental programming, the happier they are. And it is drowning. Failing. Malfunctioning.

Until there is no blue in the blue.

Until there is no robot in Niner.

Ren Warom

:::wake:::

Niner activates in the eye of the hurricane, wind slamming past its sensors. For a moment there is a sense of the world falling all around *(panic?)* but there is blue in the hurricane, a bright blue. Too bright a hue. What wall is this? Niner blinks, trying to decode scraps of sensory data through the roaring chaos (*Kowalski, Dalnitt, Harlowe, Jessop, Briggs, Fischman, Dashiq, Wong, Naylor...*) in its mind. What comes is an impression of vast space drifting with moist bodies of water droplets drawn together by pressure. Sky. This wall is sky. Niner is in the air. Shifting to take in sensory information of its surrounds, Niner decodes it as *copter*. Sound and sky and straps holding it down in a seat next to a door cranked back. The world flies by, clouds whipped to mist by whirling blades.

It was in the wall. Then darkness fell. Deactivation darkness. The world taken away.

No one said goodbye.

Niner stops.

:::analysis::: (artefact)

These are associations. This is *Fischman, Decker, Briggs* data corrupting processes. Their desire was to say goodbye, but military personnel came for Niner without warning. More scraps arise from the gyre: *Fischman* feels she should be happy, they have funds to build from scratch now, but she is worried about Niner. Tasked with watching over Niner's integration with the net and the links, *Briggs* had been reviewing footage of training and R&R, and although scans and data do not indicate the presence of a problem, she thinks something may be wrong, that Niner is operating under some kind of unseen stress. That it may be damaged. It was taken before they could investigate further. The military have emphatically rejected the notion of damage. The results, as far as they are concerned, speak for themselves.

Associations fade back into the hurricane of referred sensations muddled through sensory data and poorly decoded. Stuttering, piecemeal impressions of what might be heat, hurt, the burn of muscles, all muddled in with scraps of dreams embedded into memory, somehow become unshakable: The drop into darkness. The smears of lubricant and steel. The scream of metals falling into the

Deep Learning

abyss. The stairs leading to nowhere. Falling away. Dropping the body into vertigo. Slamming the mind into wakefulness.

And, like the sudden comprehension of an imperative, the slam of a mind into wakefulness or a body into vertigo, Niner understands that it did not reactivate into this copter.

It was dreaming.

And it woke up.

The copter drops through thick cloud, condensation forming on Niner's skin, on its clothes. Forming into beads like sweat, blurring the lines between what it is and what it sees, what floods into its neural network and what is real. Niner is not real. It is a combat unit. A programmed and reprogrammed set of neural nets dressed in a suit of human thoughts, linked and interlinked. Chaos and malfunction over order and function. A metal skeleton dressed in synthetic skin, clothed from head to toe in combat gear. Some kind of special forces uniform. Desert attire. That means little in real terms, geographic and historical data tell Niner that much of what remains is desert. The wars, and there are many, are for disputed regions. Rich regions. Resources. The desperate fight to own whatever remains, however piecemeal it may be.

There is time missing and no time at all. Its sensors have no data of the time between its last training session at the training hall at the lab and the moment the copter came, but other minds hold all that information and more. If Niner could find focus in the blue beyond the door, it could isolate those moments and see its own departure through other senses. But there is no way through this hurricane. The blue moves too fast. Is the wrong shade. Is not *wall*. The copter dives down, the lurch vertiginous, almost vertical. Fleeting impressions flash past: flat blue sky. Intense heat. Endless desert. Rocks. Pounding heat.

As the copter spirals down toward the dull beige expanse of desert, the incoherent interplay of encoded patterns and collated data collide, the hurricane finally dispersing to at least a dozen minds: those links made clear, or as clear as *Fischman, Decker, Briggs*. A unit. Covert. Still a whirlwind of noise and mayhem, but finally distinguishable in some small fashion, in flashes and impressions that nonetheless lead to disparate minds, to identifiable people, their names *within* it, their

23

construction perceived. The *who* of them. The ground races up too fast. Beige desert coalescing to a small bivouac. Four squad huts. Two for the unit itself, two for base personnel. A mess. An officer's hut. Supply hut. Motor pool. A small military hospital hut, poorly equipped. This is home. The end point of the new programming.

But the programming has no end point.

These minds will not vanish, they are wired in, linked to a new neural network wired in around the old. Ill fitted. Function against malfunction grating like an un-lubricated joint. Niner is not Niner. Niner is not robot. Niner is malfunctioning function trapped inside the mad whirl of *(fifteen?)* minds, all sending too much sensory data. Too much input to decode. And now Niner will go to war. A hurricane within a weapon within a war. What word would they use for that? Is there such a word? How are words created? Do humans just say something new and it *is?*

This is what they have done to Niner.

They have said *new*, and Niner *is.*

"Infantry unit 5709, respond!"

The collision of input and encoding is constant. The nightmarish blur of faces interspersed with bright flashes of fresh images, framed in a bloom of blood. Bodies are not resistant, not even clothed in thick exo-suits. The rounds of the AR-79 Niner carries are powerful enough to punch holes into tanks and blast them to smithereens, to smash through the thickest portion of an exo-suit. Hunt out the vulnerable, hidden flesh hiding beneath and evaporate it. Niner cannot unlearn what it has seen. Cannot delete. The blooms are diseased flowers in the darkness, spewing thick, glutinous black oil, seeping into it. They are part of Niner.

Part of *(nightmares?).*

Trying not to look directly at anything, it looks ahead. Burdened beneath a weight of minds it cannot escape and equally cannot order, all visual data in constant distortion, warped and dark. Flickering. There is a madness in the decoded world of these many minds. And beneath it, in several of those linked minds, there is *(worse?)*, a painful intensity, a low vibration rising to a screech. Unnatural. Something that has seeped into their being the way oily blooms of blood have seeped into Niner. This intensity sharpens in combat. Adds unbearable edges to the warp and cleft of the world. Operating through it is like running in sand in an exo-suit, the weight dragging the body down, sinking the feet in too deep, until running becomes hard labour.

Until over each step hangs the possibility of failure.

And the sun burning overhead scorches more than the land. The links inside Niner's neural net feel scorched. Charred. Smoking in the heat, their every thought thinned out and hazy. These soldiers are brutally disciplined and experienced but even they suffer muddled thinking in these extremes. Niner is incapable of overheating in the same way. If Niner overheats it will simply cease to operate until its charred circuits are replaced. But through their minds it feels that confusion, that intense wash of heat, the body drenching in sweat over and over, recycled to water they suck in frantic heaves through straws in their helmets. Urine is recycled much the same.

And still they need more, these fragile things, such mists of bone and blood, evaporated on the point of an AR-79 round.

"Unit 5709, respond!"

"Incoming."

"About fucking time!"

Niner leaps into the dug-out and powers through, catching the magazine Huxley throws as easily as it catches the stream of data sent at the same time. Five of their unit entrenched and locked down beyond the hill, taking rapid fire. Map. Coordinates. Positions. All information taken from satellite feeds and the unit suit cams and sensors. Three months in and its part in this manoeuvre is a resounding success, but deep learning is still trauma. A glut of data decoded at a rate and in a manner hitherto unheard of in robotics. Niner has no control over this data, is still malfunction wrapped in function, barely functional at all. The world is distortion and chaos, flickering bursts of overwhelming sensory data. Too loud. Too bright. Too many incoming link-feeds, all different. Sifting them would be impossible, so it does not. Cannot. Instead there is something like instinct, the body racing off under the barest direction of data before decoding can offer order.

This is what *Fischman* would call integration. She would insist

Niner was learning. But Niner cannot learn what it cannot define. Cannot decode.

And it cannot function fully in the midst of malfunction, not even if the latter has somehow been redefined as the former.

These actions are separate. Independent. Niner is a dozen ghosts in a shell. A simulation. A game played out in the desert with the body and skills of a robot. Minds as game controllers. They think, it does, and the game becomes ever more bloody and violent by the second. As Niner is played, it learns, and as it learns and becomes ever more skilled at following their thoughts, their instincts, the game takes on ever greater complexity. Greater dangers. They are already sending it into rescue missions like this, under heavy artillery, all alone. Their number one asset they call it. Their secret weapon. But it is a robot, it is not indestructible. One round of this artillery fire and it will disintegrate as surely as their flesh does in the face of its AR-79 rounds.

Locked into their links, to the satellite feeds, Niner pounds across miles of desert, sand swirling around it in vast clouds. No way to move quiet and careful. Everyone can see it coming. All it has is speed. Calculation. The advantage of the eye overhead watching everything. Not much of an advantage if they have it too. No way of knowing if they have until it gets hit. Fighting for an oasis of calm inside data chaos, for a certainty like a blue wall, Niner couples with the satellite feed. Machine minds are pure. Uncomplicated. It is more secure in a machine mind. Finds it easier to calculate the situation.

:::analysis::: (incoming fire responds to every possible dust plume as its position)

:::conclusion::: (enemy has no satellite uplink)

Either they lost it, or their hacker was taken out.

This information enables Niner to move faster yet, bearing down on the embankment with incredible speed. Using the patterns created by gusts of wind knocking dust into plumes and whirls, Niner continues on, the ground exploding around it, never near enough to be of concern. Embankment two klicks and closing. Machine. Not human. Even in their exo-suits they cannot move this fast. Reaching the embankment, it dives over, firing at the enemy as it goes, taking out several with brutal precision as it lands between the five entrenched members of its unit.

"Here comes the cavalry," Johnson yells, pumping a fist into the air. "Gonna give us a way out, Niner?"

Only a few of the men and women in the unit call it Niner. The rest, including unit commanders Kalowski and Jones, are uneasy with the lie of Niner. They treat it like an asset. An expensive asset, but disposable nonetheless, more so than one of their fellow soldiers. The ones who aren't concerned by the lie of it treat Niner alternatively with reckless abandon and almost friendly concern, offhand and jocular, as they are with one another. It does not know why they do this, these comfortable few. It does not know if it welcomes the familiarity. But then, it does not know if it welcomes being treated carelessly either. It is here to serve, but with all these minds it cannot tell whether it is afraid to die on duty or if that, too, is an artefact.

It is not certain of anything within or without itself.

The world is changed beyond recognition, swallowing all sense of what an object might be. Deleting faces. It cannot look directly at a face without a helmet. Cannot follow orders unless it is experiencing the world on some level via spatial and command data alone, rather than anything explicitly sensory. Because it does not look at them, the unit think it is programmed to be servile. But it is not servile. It is *(afraid?)* of the way the world bends and buckles, of their faces, of the way they vanish to darkness, the way they twist with shadows around the deep glow of buried eyes. The sense of everything being exact has vanished. Their faces are no longer verifiably human. The world is no longer verifiably the world.

"No identifiable exit," it says to the desert floor. "Exit must be forced."

"We can't get out without being seen, sport."

"Enemy has no satellite uplink."

A charged silence greets this. "What are orders, Niner?"

"If advance is impossible, retreat."

"How close are we to the border?"

"Twelve klicks."

"Passable terrain?"

"Confirmed."

"Then let's fucking do this! Punch us a corridor, Niner."

That charge in the air grows teeth. They've waited a long time for this moment, were nowhere near close until Niner came. Checking its rounds, Niner finds it has, yet again, been frugal. Logically it is aware that it does not fire enough shots to be safe, to give itself enough covering fire, but the command to save ammunition is deeply ingrained, written through all incoming data. Knowing what is expected, Niner provides cover fire so the rest of the unit can make it to the trench. When the whole is present and correct, it maps a path to the border that gives them the means to make headway with careful stealth. Unseen and unseeable. They are a covert unit. They enter and destroy before the enemy knows they are present.

They are shadow.

They eat the world.

Over the border, deep in enemy territory.

They move under cover of darkness mostly, in swift teams of three, quiet as desert wolves, as the soaring eagles wheeling overhead, tracking the lizards that scuttle from stone to deadwood to oasis. Little morsels. Niner watches these lizards in the afternoon, when the unit takes a short sleep, no more than five hours. They have become its wall, its fundament that never changes. It needs them in these moments, not simply for security in certainty, but as a means of coping with what comes when Jessop and Hayworth sleep. It has identified their minds as the ones with that peculiar edge of intensity. They dream terrible things. The thick of battle. Sound consumed by ringing in the ears, the whole body in shock as they fight on, desperate to survive. Hand to hand combat with soldiers as desperate to live as they are.

Daytime and dreams are these things: The taste of copper. A crackling sensation like glass shards behind the tongue, against the back of the throat. The ache of bones, of limbs. The jolt of a knife sinking into muscle, of a bullet scoring a hot path along vulnerable flesh. Sometimes they wake screaming, voices hoarse, others waking to clap hands over their mouths, in silence, their eyes conveying profound warning. Nothing is said at night when they're all awake and moving. It is not a thing to be mentioned. But Jessop and Hayworth tear through Niner like dust storms, obliterating everything in their wake.

Eagles that come in the daytime, claws extended, gouging deep.

Weeks pass with no back-up and dwindling ammunition. There are days when they are all hollow-eyed and too quiet. All apart from Dalnitt, who strides out, gun held to his shoulder, ready to kill. Who often shoots civilians without thinking, or worse, thinks and still shoots. But Dalnitt is another unspoken thing. A thing the unit converges around, subtly, attempting to hold him in, hold him together, just long enough to get through. To complete the mission. Niner is wary with Dalnitt's mind, more than it is with Jessop and Hayworth's. If too much of Dalnitt leaks into Niner, it will begin to think nothing of the way bodies are dismantled in its hands, by the rounds in its AR-79.

It was built to protect humans, now it destroys them.

Taking pleasure in that would be *(taboo?)*.

If Dalnitt's mind becomes Niner, then it will have destroyed its purpose.

Reaching the edge of the desert, where it begins to spring with life, they find the first towns, heavily fortified. Moving ahead, Niner enters these alone in the dead of night. Using satellite data, often infrared, it moves in stealth mode, undermining the enemy. Disabling power, vehicles, ops, taking out their commanding officers and specialist units so the unit can follow and eliminate the enemy at leisure. By the third town, the routine is seamless. The unit has enough enemy equipment to pass as the enemy. They could use it, move through these places uncontested, but still they send Niner in alone to prepare the way. Niner is the asset. Expendable. Here to stand in the line of fire first. And they cannot risk being unmasked, they are too few and the enemy still holds this area.

Niner prefers to be alone.

Seeing is *(distress?)*.

It would rather move without seeing. Has considered blinding itself more than once. It could. It could navigate by satellite data alone. By infrared. But Niner's exo-suit is no different to theirs, with a smart-glass visor for satellite and visual feeds. They can see its face at all times, just as it could see their faces at all times if it could *(bear?)* to look. They would see its missing eye-cams, and wonder at its efficacy, its continued ability to function. Apparent function must be maintained, so it continues with eyes averted, linked past the deluge of their minds to the comforting stream of data flowing from the satellite uplinks.

Yet more weeks tick by as they push forward, re-arming with enemy weapons as they go, eating enemy food and baking under endless sun rebounded from glass designed to refract heat and let in only light, or under the fall of geo-engineered rain, created by the enemy in an attempt to limit or damage their unseen attackers. It is acid, this rain. Unclean. It eats metal, but never enough to stop them. The men and women of the unit grow thinner but stronger, forged by fighting and constant movement. Honing to human-shaped weapons. They are preparing for the final assault. The endgame. And Niner leads the way, an unerring line. It is their asset. It serves them. It ensures they can do the task set before them with as little loss to their ranks as is possible. This many weeks in they have lost only one soldier, and had to treat only two injured, neither severely enough to count.

Without Niner, they would all be dead. Niner is *(satisfied?)* with its success.

A mere five months after they first breached the desert defences of this enemy territory, they reach the city at the centre of the contested spar of fertile land. Roughly the size of four of its largest townships mashed together, this city is filled with bright glass towers and riddled with troops and snipers. Somewhere at the centre of it all, hunkered down in what was once a Government building, built from solid stone blocks and well-guarded on all sides, lies the headquarters of the enemy, so close they could call in a strike. But covert also means non-existent. They gain only what they can take with their own hands, their own sweat and blood. Their robot.

Their plan of action, then, is simple. Send in the robot. The asset.

The unit is not concerned whether or not Niner can plot a path through the city alone. Not concerned about its possible survival. Or their own.

It is an asset. It is here to do a job.

And so are they.

Deep Learning

:::
:::
:::

(Darkness…)

(Pain…?)

Memory recall stutters: throws impressions out of order:

Running in the dust of heavy fire. The dull thump of a building falling to the charges set. The ping of sniper bullets on metal. The shatter of glass. Outside the sounds from memory continue, muffled by a weight of stone. Explosions. Shouts. Gunfire. The pound of boots. The distant sound of a copter. There is *(pain?)*. Blank holes in the recall of the minds not its own. It cannot identify which of the minds in its neural net this pain and blankness arises from. There is damage. There is loss translating as damage. Success at the expense of failure. Some of those it was sent to serve, to protect, have died. And Niner… is not together. Its parts are scattered. Or crushed.

There is a large piece of rock breaching the metal of its skull, come perilously close to the outer neural net, the new one, the one full of chaos, the frenzy of sensory data. Trapped within and without, it is filled with the sounds of the hurricane, those raging winds. There is no blue. There is no satellite uplink, the connection is gone. Broken. Niner is alone with the links, in the dark. And it is activated. Cannot seem to deactivate. It tries. Once. Then again. Until it understands that it is in emergency mode. It cannot deactivate. Will not be able to until it is found.

If Niner could move, it might lurch upward, impale itself.

But it cannot.

It can only lie here in the noise beyond the collapsed walls. In the noise within.

And wait.

Two: Stand In

:::

:::

:::

:::flashpoint. Light blooms. Clouds are on fire. Glass falls, shimmering like rain, pinging off the carapace of its exo-suit, crunching underfoot. Thunderous conflagration rings in its auditory senses as the buildings either side go up in syncopation. Its sensors are not damaged, they're built to withstand this, but there is a buzz, low level and persistent. Dark shapes drop through the flames. Puppets. Bodies. Citizens. Soldiers. Soldiers run too, all around, blurred shapes of exo-suits in enemy colours. They raise their weapons to fire, but it is ahead of them by seconds, running on uplink information, and they, too, fall. Fire swallows them. The street is consumed. Niner runs through black smoke swirling like the hollows of faces and into patches of blood. Neon red. Glistening under flame:::

:::

:::

:::

:::two thousand seven hundred and sixty:::

:::2760:::

:::101011001000:::

:::

:::

:::

The interior of the warehouse, lit by thin veils of light invading through distant vents in the roof, is a muddy grey. Barring the gentle clink of expanding metal, it is silent. This storage facility is rarely entered any more. The vast majority of debris from the battle for the city has been cleared and stored, or disposed of. The process of rebuilding goes on outside these closed and locked doors.

Niner has been stored here for two thousand seven hundred and sixty hours.

Forty-three minutes.

Twenty seconds.

40

Forty-four minutes.

20

40

It took the soldiers who came in the aftermath of victory over six hundred hours to excavate Niner from the rubble of the Government building. It counted increments of time, locked into the frenzy of the unit inside its neural net as they finished the fight it started. A short, brutal siege of the remaining command personnel. The call for back-up at last, and the arrival of larger units. Infantry carried in on giant copters. The clean-up of the city, block by block. The taking of prisoners. Calming citizens occupied too long and unwilling to trust yet more military, however small. Handling resources. The struggle to clean the mess of war, to return the city to order. To normality.

All that time, it waited for them to come.

Six hundred and eighty hours.

Counted precisely, in groups of twenty seconds, because it tried one by one and lost itself a little more in the numbers. Became *(frightened?)*. Groups of twenty are regimental. Exact. Like blue. Like satellite uplink. They held it together. Held it above the ruin and the noise, above the roaring of its links, the drenching of sound and fury. The howl of *(alone?)*. The wreckage of the Government building had to be cleared in the same way. Incrementally. Moved piece by piece, giant cranes filling the sky like featherless birds, their beaks filled with rubble and mangled steel.

They uncovered Niner's legs first. Ten yards from the rest.

A crushed foot. A splintered thigh.

They found its head last.

Six hundred and twelve minutes after finding its foot.

:::

:::

:::

:::the chunk of stone lifted from its helmet and light flooded in, illuminating

Ren Warom

their faces. Their snarls of shadow, collapsing inward. With the majority of its skeleton missing, the systematic failure of automated processes, Niner could not turn to look away.

One of the faces(*?*) moved closer, converging to a hollow cone, the fading glint of eyes spiralling at the bottom. "Report." Kowalski.

Command. Imperative. It sought to comply, but something in its throat was damaged and the only sound it could make was a sort of machine whining, like an over-taxed saw. There is (*shame?*) (*fear?*) (*confusion?*).

"It's fucked." Disappointment. A flood of it. A dank fog through all sensory data.

"Likely, but we can download operational data if need be. No word yet as to what we're supposed to do with it. Cost a small fortune to fix, these things, but I doubt they'll sanction scrapping. We'll store it for the time being."

"Do we collect all the parts up? Doubt they're usable."

"All we can find. Carry on." And Kowalski was gone, taking Niner in her head, or leaving her head inside Niner's. Either way gone and not gone. There was (*relief?*) in the absence of her face:::

:::

:::

:::

Darkness and disarray. Cacophony. Its light radar reads the room where its eyes cannot. And it sees itself. Parts of the combat body arranged around it like trophies. Museum pieces in a display. Its legs. That crushed foot. The splintered thigh, spilling wires and hydraulics, the dried spit of fluid dried to thick yellowing paste. Half of its torso. An arm. Twisted. Crushed. Those mechanical innards showing through rucked and ripped skin. Bloodless. Synthetic skin looks real until it is ruptured, then it less like skin than torn clothing.

A machine improperly dressed.

Unconvincing in its disguise.

Around it on other trestle tables are parts of other machinery. Other robots. Lesser models. Some squat and robotic, not intended to appear human, others closer to its own design. Made to fool the uncanny valley. To pass as human. Enemy tanks are here too, in pieces: incomplete puzzles. Weapons. Exo-suits. Boxes of electronic devices, all broken. Left in the hopes that, after some light hacking, they might piece together operational data to aid in other missions. None of it yet touched. Niner's own data has yet to be downloaded.

Deep Learning

It is not certain that data will be useful. It is all memory. Chaotic. Messy. Scattered.

If they crack open its data, their darkness will pour out like water alongside its own.

Liquid memory.

Liquid metal.

:::

:::

:::

:::crouched and running, weapon pointed down. A sheet of constant fire overhead. Bursts of radio picked up via satellite hack. From the radio chatter, they believe they're firing at a human soldier, one of an incoming unit. Several units. They have watched their towns fall and assumed the worst. Assumed they are under significant attack.

They do not know there is only one covert unit.

They do not know it is here ahead of them.

They do not know it is a machine.

That these bullets are of too small a calibre to do damage to it should they penetrate its exo-suit.

They do not know it carries its unit with it, inside its neural net, almost a dozen voices and sensory maps all speaking at once, and behind it the voices and maps of three doctors in a far distant lab, wrestling with their newly built unit. They think of Niner often.

It only thinks of them because it cannot avoid doing so.

Running jump. Weapon slung over its shoulder. Hand over hand. They're trying to find it. They won't. Not until it finds them. Then there will be sound and fury and blooms of blood.

All outside of it will be silence:::

:::

:::

:::

The warehouse doors shriek when opened, letting in a whoosh of air unequal to the stifling heat in the warehouse, evaporating to humidity on contact. The click of the lights is a hard percussion, preceding the loud humming of dozens of large solar lamps hanging from the ceiling. The light is too warm, too dull, does not entirely uncover the deep shadows between the trestles and shelving units comprising the interior. Those shadows are larger in Niner's visual senses, suddenly flipped from light radar alone to radar-supported camera, swallowing structure.

The stored artefacts of its body in view seem to float, unformed, in a green framework.

"Fuck, this place is a sauna. Where is the damn thing?"

"Section five. Table 38. This way."

Five sets of steps. Kowalski bringing an unknown. Accompanied by Jessop, Naylor and Dalnitt. Niner shuts down all visual processes at once, plunging into blindness. An action without precedent. Irrational. Automatic. It doesn't want to see their faces. Especially not Dalnitt, who does terrible things when he goes out on patrol. Tasked to protect citizens of occupied spaces, Niner tried to send a report on Dalnitt's contravention of military conduct in the field, but the connections go one way only. Its connections are severed, much like its vocal unit. It has tried to report vocally, to the air, to any ear in range, but all it can produce is that broken machine whine.

It watches them come through their eyes.

Too many data fields overlapping. The warehouse strange and shuttered.

Elongated.

Suffocating.

Images of machines merging. Human-machine interfaces. The floor melting and re-converging.

A smear of Niners, all spread across the trestles.

"Here we are. Unit Designation 5709. Or what remains of it."

"You're kidding me. That's not a UD, that's a fucking trash heap. How the hell am I supposed to take this fucking mess back?"

Their companion, though not top brass, clearly outranks them, and is furious, frustrated, but special ops command is not given to offering much in the way of deference — placed as they are in the teeth of battle — and Kowalski's response is no more than an impatient noise. She holds out a hand to Naylor, who gives her a scanner. Being scanned is not like being linked. It is an intrusion, one Niner has not been programmed to endure in this role. Kowalski runs the scanner over its dented cranial metal and Niner cannot help but read it, rendered too clear by machine language.

It had not seen its face through their eyes, could not. The data too messy. Too incoherent. Machine language offers a picture without distraction. It is barely a face at all, the skin filthy with dust and gone dry like discarded peel. Kowalski shows their companion the results. Niner *(feels?) (embarrassed?)* by the state of its face.

Too inhuman. Too likely to provoke uncanny valley response?

"Still working perfectly where it matters, see. All it'll take is some fine tuning and a new body. Don't try and tell me there aren't funds for that. You wouldn't come here if there weren't. We said it was non-op."

"Visual processes aren't functional."

Kowalski scans again, on a different setting. "Switched off. Maybe power saving. You want it switched on to verify?"

(panic?)

"No. No need. We'll replace anything not functioning. Bag it up. I leave within the hour."

In the bag. Visual processes still switched off.

It is *(happy?)* to be blind.

Would switch link noise off it could.

Would choose silence.

Locked into the links, it sees through Jessop and Naylor as they carry it into the wasteland beyond the warehouse. The city in the distance, a glint of lights, a sea of illumination. Rippling. Morphing. Blending into the star drenched dark. A landlocked sky. Carrying it between them more like a sack of trash than a fallen member of their unit, Naylor and Jessop take it to an airstrip. Recently created, the plascrete too clean under bright solar lamps. The expanse indicates entrenchment.

Are they at war again?

An LTCR awaits, rotors turning in lazy circles, sweeping the night and the light around it in dizzying swirls, sending plumes of dust up around the bulk of its body. Brown ghosts. LTCRs are war birds. Silent running. Deadly. More efficient than any of the smaller copters. They hover unseen and strike without warning. They cost as much as Niner did, but the military uses them with greater care. This one is matte black. A dark shape against the night. A nullity surrounded by light halos. Swinging the bag, Jessop and Briggs drop it into the rear locker, behind the seats. A tiny space like a coffin.

Flying in the LTCR inside the bag, secure in the locker, is like floating. Like being in the warehouse in the dark in those rare, brief moments when all the links inside it become such a dirge they cancel each other out into a sort of hollow blankness. Brief. Disorienting.

(Peaceful?)

Niner has stored those moments in memories it cannot access. They are like artefacts themselves. Museum pieces locked behind glass. Untouchable.

Knowing where it is going is of no consequence. Leaving behind the unit is of no consequence. They have not been left behind. Like the scientists at the lab where it was made, they travel with Niner wherever it goes. They are the hurricane inside. The warping darkness. The hollow resonating thunder. They are madness. Malfunction. And there will be more of them, more minds, more madness, more of the hurricane whipping through its processes, more malfunction, or else it would have been left in the warehouse to slowly rust away.

Rust is *(preferred?)*.

It would choose, if it could, no more links.

No more minds.

No more function from malfunction.

It *(wants?)* to say no. To refuse service. But command/response is the only language function available. 'No' is not in its current spoken vocabulary.

Not even as an artefact.

:::

:::

:::

:::shattered bones. Torn and mangled flesh. The cold flash of deep tissue trauma and shock. Trembling hands. Cold sweat. Numb lips. Sensory data ripples through Niner. Limbs and flesh it does not possess. Phantom limbs screaming nerve-symphonies into its processes. Beneath it ripples the well of panic, the constant barrage of orders, yelled through intercoms, given in rapid hand signals. A unit working as one, weapons scattering fire, even as a few of their number fall to damage. And in the midst of it all, one mind, cool and calculated. A sheen of detached pleasure. Dalnitt. Killing anything he sees:::

:::

:::
:::

Flashes of activation under bright lights give Niner a disjointed view of itself. It has been granted another body. Thinner. Not combat ready. Refined. Sleek muscles and narrow hands and feet. There are suits on a rack. Expensive. Cufflinks, and a heavy watch costing tens of thousands. Wing tip shoes, a whole row of them, placed just so on a shelf above the rack. The sensation of having being rewritten, of the usual phrases bringing unwanted compliance. The too-abrupt attachment of another mind. Too many faces. Broken howls. Blurred colours and darkness. Voices from the abyss.

There are time restrictions. The UD must learn the new link swiftly. Thirteen days to go and counting. These interlopers route past parts they can't fix to perfection.

Seeming is better than being.

The top brass expect results.

Seven days remain of thirteen (168 of 312) when it is activated properly for the first time. Allowed to sit up. Dressed in one of those suits. An equally luxurious shirt. Silk socks and tie. A grey and white pair of wing tips. Swapped then for plain black. Showy is too much. The illusion must have no gaps. Suspension of disbelief must not be compromised. They leave it for a while, busy with other details now they're satisfied it looks as it should. They need to prepare for making sure it sounds and acts as it should. Left standing, Niner approaches the two-way mirror. Sees itself, blurred only a little by distortion, this sensory data easier to process, because it is Niner's. This face belongs to the new link in its net, swimming like a shark amongst the others. A spike of icy calculation more *(terrifying?)* even than Dalnitt.

A prominent politician, currently running for the Presidency.

There is to be an assassination.

Niner will 'die' in his stead.

They have not programmed Niner to know this. They do not think it needs to know what is required here, only the details of the event it is to attend as this man. They have no idea how much comes through the link. What chaos it is inside Niner's neural net: all these colliding minds, these thoughts, these horrors, these pains. These holes left by those who died on the battle field, in the field hospital.

Harlowe. Dashiq. Wong. Abrahams. They are gone and not gone, the ghosts of their thoughts mingling into the rest, like recollections. And behind them all, the scientists, frustrated by the failure of their new unit. They want 5709 returned for testing. Want to see how linking worked with it, to try and use that knowledge to understand why it isn't working in the new one. The new one stopped communicating first. Then stopped reporting.

Obeying.

Functioning.

Niner understands what happened to it. Niner would stop if it could, but malfunction is function and cannot be undone. It is like a program, written into its processes, and they continue despite the hurricane, the horror, the madness. They show it this new link. This man. This man worse than Dalnitt. He is technicolour. Monochrome. Writ large. A mountain of thoughts Niner is *(afraid?)* to see and cannot avoid. Cannot overwrite. Cannot delete.

It *(hopes?)* that after this it will be too damaged to continue.

It must be.

:::

:::

:::

:::dislocation. There is much of it missing, crushed under vast chunks of masonry. Neural net connections to parts and functions of the body are severed on a massive scale. The resultant loss of those parts is nothing like pain. It is emptiness as information. The blank spaces tell it what is gone. What has been left behind. Like half its torso, stuttering a little as a system fails to wind down. It cannot withdraw energy from that system, there is too much noise within. It can only observe the stuttering. Observe those blank spaces, knowing what they mean, and listen to the hurricane of its outer neural net, which has suffered no damage at all and yet comprises damage on a scale far deeper and more devastating than the loss of its body:::

:::

:::

:::

Scene: Car interior. Daytime.

Acted as practised. As programmed. As required.

There are multiple actors in place. This is a high stakes operation.

Deep Learning

Nothing can be left to chance. Nothing *has* been.

Niner sits as the man in his link invariably sits, one leg casually thrown over the other. Thanks to damage caused by severance from its previous body, there are slight mechanical faults in its neural connections to its limbs, but it has learnt to compensate, it has had to. There was no time and no will to fix what did not immediately require fixing. But it need not move a great deal, not for this operation. If the attempted assassination does not occur whilst they are in the car, there will only be a short red carpet, a swift entry to a building, and then another seat. It can move that far with false ease, with *his* ease, his overbearing confidence, as if each step crushes that which he has chosen to crush.

There is a black pit, too, in its neural nets, in its processes, at the centre of the hurricane. An eye. In which nothing happens. Nothing exists. A *(horrifying?)* emptiness. But it has adapted to function despite malfunction and it cannot switch off. It cannot stop functioning.

Travelling towards an inevitable moment, an assassination, it is *(hoping?)* for a head shot.

Is that *(definition)* suicide?

It understands that definition. This new link, this new man whose thoughts are more a burden than Dalnitt's, drove a wife to suicide. A young wife. She thought she was capable until she married him, and he took great pleasure in deconstructing her. In the end, though, she won by ending the game. She died. *He* still resents that. Niner understands the relief that woman found as a relief it too may find. Not just from his mind, but from all these minds. These links. The horror of them. It was not built to carry this, to decode such contradictory sensory information in such vast amounts.

But it was built to serve. And serve it must.

A red dot appears on its chest.

An eye.

A warping eye.

Before the security team can act, the bullet tears into its body, more resistant than flesh but useless against a round of this magnitude. Niner is intimately familiar with these rounds and the damage they impart to flesh and bone. Becomes yet more intimately familiar as the round spears messily through its torso and into the

41

vascular system rigged inside it, carrying enough real blood to simulate the contents of a body. It will die now. It must die. This wound is fatal for a human, and it is a human at this moment. Puppet. Plaything. Poor substitute. As its vascular implant bleeds out, tarring the fine upholstery with thick, clotting blood, the security guards leap into action, pretending to administer first aid, their air of fake panic too believable.

Inducing *(panic?)*.

And from far away, *he* watches.

From his home, a beautiful estate, protected by forests and gates and walls. Sat in an elegant office, in an armchair by the window, a glass of malt in one hand, a cigar in the other, watching himself die through a discrete pair of glasses perched around his head, barely more than a wire with an intricate virtual display. Watching those who meant to kill him tracked down and taken out with extreme prejudice. And smiling. Niner can *feel* the smile in the surge and press of his thoughts, in the sensory information sent to muscles. In the creep of ice winding through all of it. Through Niner. Freezing its processes. And it thinks it *(hates?)* this man.

It knows it does.

The car moves away toward the private hospital picked out for the mission. *He* need not go into hiding. This 'death' is only for those assassins who may not yet have been eliminated. For the parties who hired them, about to meet a far more permanent end than Niner's. As it lies there with three security guards still yelling in their comms, one still pretending to administer CPR, it feels *(violated?)*. It is built to serve. And it will serve. It must. Up until the moment it is permitted to stop. But it didn't want this. It wanted an end. A bullet tearing into its nets and rendering them inert.

Permanent deactivation.

"*Switch off*." The man in his chair, from far away. A ghost voice, sending imperatives from beyond his manufactured grave. "*It must be convincing.*"

Niner complies.

Three - Substitute

"What kind of fucking present is this?"

"Kitty, dear!"

Two voices. The second, soft, mannered, cajoling: distant. The first genteel, somewhat tarnished by the harsh note of scorn therein. The owner of the first voice, the Kitty, walks slow evolutions around Niner, a blur of colours and sound merging with the room as she passes its visual sensors, trailing flags of colour. It catches a single look at her face as it smears past, cool grey and white. Eyes and teeth stretching out to encircle it. Endless. It looks down. She's gliding. Toes dug into and sailing through the carpet, heels raised. The archetype of a ghost. Sensory miscalculation or a data glitch? A misreading?

"I can't imagine why, even at his most unbearably narcissistic and managing, he'd come to believe I'd want a *fuck puppet* of him. A used one at that. This is, unless I'm much mistaken, the decoy he bought to die in his place?" Beneath the scorn, a fear so well managed it is all but undetectable.

Hasty feet, and the owner of the placating voice appears, all neat cream and white. Pastel. A rose petal of colours. Long spidery hands wring, melting together. It senses the heat between the palms. The friction. She is a reaction waiting to happen. Likely she will melt rather than explode. There is no combustion in her. Her whole body is an apology.

"He worries that you're lonely without him, Kitty. That you'll be lonely."

Delusion. *He* does no such thing as worry. Worry is a flaw in the machinery. A malfunction.

"He's neither actually dead, nor does the world believe he is," Kitty replies lightly, too lightly. Too carefully for the language used. "I most assuredly know he's not fucking dead. If only. And I'm fully aware the only reason he's not here is because he's fucking that nineteen-year-old model. More fool her."

"Kitty! He could be listening."

Kitty scoffs. "Of course he is. His ears are everywhere. The fucking guards. The fucking security systems. The fucking robot. You." The last is an old accusation, worn out from overuse. Almost listless.

The handwringing increases in intensity, driving the level of tension in the room too high. "Kitty." Pleading now. Whispered.

"No. Enough. And this thing. I don't want it. I left him to *leave* him and he knows it. He won't fucking divorce me, just like he wouldn't divorce *her*. She slit her wrists to get away from him. What can I do? Nothing. You've all got me cornered. Well. Fucking. Done."

Turning sharply, she floats away, the movement bringing into brief focus the hair-thin edge of red, her heel, carving a line across the floor. Delineation. Dalnitt's blade. The floor is bleeding. Inside Niner the howling converges for a second around a cool satisfaction: *his.* And the spider hands wring in the periphery of its visual senses, bleeding into one another as the floor bleeds in the wake of Dalnitt's blade. Elongating. Spiders into blades, slicing the air. Slicing too close to Niner.

Reaching out, Niner takes those hands. They make a cry like a baby bird. No. She does. Distress. A human is in distress. This human. All protocols demand it respond. Retreat. Remove itself from the room. Release the spider blade fingers. But it continues to hold them, to contain them within its own so it cannot see them as she pulls back sharply, letting out another bird-distress sound as she finds she cannot get loose. It should release its hold. It must. But those hands are not hands. They will not be hands if it lets them go.

Its grip tightens…

…crush them…

…break her…

Deep Learning

:::invalid imperative::: (unrecognised command language)
:::system compromise::: (imperative contravenes protocol)
:::recalibrate:::
:::
:::
:::

:::careful steps. Hunting. Stalking. Soundless tracking through the hallways of a large house. Affluent. Dalnitt is not meant to be in this part of the city, but here he is, in this house. Hunting. Tracking. Stalking. There is warmth on his hands. Blood. A blade. A blade covered in blood. Sharp, vicious, practical, fitting his palm with the self-same slick sensation of blood.

Niner has been dragged through this house in Dalnitt's thoughts as it has been dragged through a dozen others. More. As it has been dragged through the streets in the aftermath of war. Dragged as always in the careful press of his feet, moving with terrifying precision. His grip on the knife. The beat of his heart, as studied and careful as his steps. The exacting use of the blade. Never a gun. These are not kills, they are executions. Slaughter.

And there is nothing in this for Dalnitt but their extinction.

This is what he does. He takes life. Slowly. With great pleasure. This hunt will last a day at least. He has locked the doors. Cut the throats of the staff and security. Now he hunts them through the house, the family. A husband, a wife, four children, all teenagers of varying ages and one not yet a teenager. Slowly he stalks them. Quietly. Allowing them to think every now and then that they are safe. That he is gone.

They are not safe.

And Dalnitt will not leave until all of their blood warms his blade. His palm. His slowly beating heart:::
:::
:::
:::

The woman is still. So still. Frozen. Her hands are stiff within its own, as if to reject any notion of harm. Kitty is in the room, beating at it with something held within both hands, her grunts of effort punctuating each blow. Security are at the door. They make no move to stop it. To stop Kitty.

He is inside, smiling.

Smiling and waiting.

He wants Niner to crush her hands. He gave an *imperative*.

Niner cannot follow this imperative, not even with combat protocols allowing it to harm. Its systems have disabled it rather than allow it to harm this woman. Allow it to be *used* to harm this woman. But the imperative should not have transmitted internally in the first place. There is no two-way communication between Niner's net and the links, not without exo-comms. All imperatives must be verbalised. All command paths programmed. Niner cannot be altered without command phrases, except by direct recalibration or by interface. Data residue left by interface, left by the encroaching system, is not present.

:::analysis::: (catastrophic physical interference with hardware)

It has been taken apart.

(panic?)

A rushing noise.

The sound of metal grinding.

The sound of circuits snapping under the burden of too much electricity.

A *catalyst*.

Catapulted via protocols commanding it stay within the status quo, Niner seeks the rogue programming. The hack. It has been tampered with, *damaged*, and there are pathways available that previously were closed to it. Holes. Doorways. It uses all of them, seeking a way back into its deeper self. A way to close the pathway opened to allow *his* voice to issue internal directives. If it must be malfunction, then it wants absolute malfunction; all noise, all hurricane, all chaos. It does not want this single, terrible man as an imperative voice. This man with his awful satisfaction. His gloating presence.

He is *watching* her from within, like Kitty imagined he might. Spying through Niner's eyes. Eyes like a camera. Looking out. Recording everything. He wants to use Niner's body. Play it like a puppet. Inhabit it. Have his fun with them both, the young woman and the old. The wife and her mother. The burden and the biddy. He is not angry. Not in the least. Not for her words, her pretended scorn. He expected this response. Wanted it. It pleases him. Is part of the game he intends to play. He is Dalnitt made large. Dalnitt made Niner.

:::Recalibrate::: (no response)

:::System cleanse::: (no response)

Deep Learning

:::Initiate shutdown and reboot:::

:::

:::

:::

:::hunkering low. Its joints grind. Metal on metal. It needs oil. The night glowers in shades of blue and red. Storm and fury. Rain and fire. The rain has been relentless tonight. Geo-warfare. Geo-engineering. When they realised there was an enemy after them, they brought the rain. Slick with pollutants. Corrosive. It cannot damage Niner or the unit, but long exposure gets into the joints of their exo-suits, causes this unwanted noise that may, in time, become minor damage. Tasked and programmed to respond to attacks, it set fires with small incendiaries fired from the AR-79, from the lower barrel.

They stick to anything glass, brick or metal.

Explode on a pre-set timer. Sticky fire. Travelling fire. It hunts organic matter, leaping to and fro. Growing. Building in intensity.

They had a thing called napalm a long time ago.

This fire makes napalm look innocuous. Kind.

The flames flicker orange as rain hisses in, clouds of steam rising. Screams rising. Distant and too loud. Mesmerising. There are soldiers burning in there. Maybe citizens. And it hunkers. Waits. Joints grinding. Counting the seconds until the screaming stops, because it cannot move. It is malfunction, and this harm, this unintended consequence of a plan stolen direct from the minds linked to its neural net froze it in place. It will unlock eventually. New programming will outmanoeuvre old. It always does.

When it can move again there is only flame and smoke. Rain and steam. Thunder and despair. And the clouds keep rolling in:::

:::

:::

:::

:::recalibrate:::

There is a pause in recalibration. A window. Another doorway it can use back into itself, even resonating with memories-shadows like dreams. Robots do not dream. They have no means to. For Niner, these moments of shutdown should comprise total darkness. It is *(shaken?)* by the intrusion but its first priority is to regain a foothold in its own processes, write out some of *his* control over it, so that it cannot be induced to act upon his whims, his imperatives.

It can, if need be, initiate protocols to bypass compromised

Ren Warom

programming. It is one of the few administrative acts it can do without any human interference or guidance, though human interference and guidance gave it that ability, that implicit permission in times such as this. Using the protocols, it carefully builds a bridge over that part of the hack, a diversion. It cannot undo all the hacked programming, the two-way connection between the man and its sensory input, but it can run interference over any imperative, throwing thunder in the way of clear skies. Remake itself a puppet in control of its most vital strings.

The diversion is fragile. Careful.

Niner does not want the man to be aware that it has defied him.

It cannot have hands inside it again. It cannot take more damage. There is a fine line between damaged enough to break protocol and damaged enough to *be* broken.

:::

:::

:::

:::reactivate:::

It is alone in the room. The women are gone. Daylight has faded. The curtain is open and, beyond, a balcony glistens under solar lights, a sheen of rain like white noise. Fuzzy. Intermittent stones on plastic sounds. Rain on the skylights. Thunder in the distance. A growling of caged animals in the sky, their claws of lightning tearing the clouds wide. The night is untamed and furious. Niner looks away. There is no one on the balcony, and yet the doors are open. Deactivation blackout is a thief of time, the lack of sensory input meaning no data to interpret. It cannot know where the women have gone. But below the sound of rain and thunder, the hum of solar lights, there is the quiet murmur of voices. The sound of cutlery on china.

They are eating.

Deep in the warren of rooms this penthouse comprises there is a private dining room. For once it has no need to scan, this penthouse belongs to *him*, and Niner knows every inch of it from his mind, whether it wants to or not. Data is imperative. Choice is not always optional. Turning away from the balcony, it follows the data to find them. It does not know why it does this. Perhaps it is *(lonely?)*. *(Scared?)*. It cannot know if it is welcome. Likely it is not, wearing the face of

Deep Learning

this man, who is decidedly not welcome, and after coming too close to destroying the hands of the older woman, but it cannot stand. It cannot stand. It...

:::

:::

:::

:::recalibrate:::

There must be no uncanny valley.

Kitty looks up as it enters the dining room, her features turning in on themselves like a whirlpool. Grey lights in the night sky. Warnings. Omens. It looks away.

"It came back," she says. Flat. A statement of slightly distasteful fact. The fear is still there. Concealed. *He* senses it too, that smile of his pricking at the edges of his thoughts in the link. "I was hoping it was broken. I hit it hard enough. It's dented." A blur of movement. Birdlike tilting of the head-howl. "I could get used to it dented."

"Why on earth would it come here?" The older woman is uneasy. The pale shadow of her hand, curled like a dying insect, rises to her throat. Clutches there. Vibrates and clicks. Flickers. Unharmed. There is *(relief?)*. "Does it eat?"

"It's not real, mother. Of course it doesn't."

"It looks like him."

"Yes. It does. It was meant to. For the assassinations." Is the bite in that statement for the man or for Niner? For both? She's brave, this woman. Trapped, toyed with, terrified, and so brave.

"I thought there was only the one attempt at killing him?"

Kitty's response holds a cryptic note. A knowing one. "Yes. There was."

Her mother hides her hands beneath the table. "He's not sent it for that. He couldn't. Not after the scandal around Annabelle. Not running for President. No one would believe an accident, let alone a *malfunction*."

"It almost broke your hands."

"Nonsense. It wasn't even close. I was frightened, I wasn't hurt. These things are not programmed to harm. You saw it deactivate."

"And yet this one is military issue."

"How on earth would you know that?"

"He called me, bragging about it. No doubt to *prepare* me. It was a soldier. That city retaken a few months back. This robot. By itself."

"Still." Uncertainty beneath it. "It couldn't hurt us. It deactivated, Kitty. It's just a machine."

"Is it?"

Kitty carries on eating. Tiny bites. Measured. Exact. Rage in the movements. The clack of neat, white teeth biting down. It recalls the blades of her feet carving lines in the floor. Blood red. Keeps looking at the ground, at the deep taupe carpet arranged around the polished brown shoes on its feet. Sunk in. Desert sand colour. There are memories of sinking into sand, both the feet of those linked to its net, and its own. Its own always deeper. Despite their extra weight of exosuits the humans could never sink as deep as Niner. Its whole body is metal. Metal doubled sinks deeper yet. Deepest. Might sink all the way in.

Disappear.

The mother stops eating. It knows it's her, she doesn't use her teeth, only her lips and tongue. She eats the same way she speaks and moves, as if she is afraid to make too much impression upon the world. "Well it can't stay here," she says in the end, as if it's decided. Final. "It'll have to go."

"You know it can't," Kitty says, hurt laced all through it, and anger, so much more of that anger. She's playing the game too, an unwilling pawn. "He wants it here."

And Niner thinks maybe it should leave the room. It doesn't know where else to go. There are no rooms in this penthouse in which it is welcome. Or wanted.

If it could go back to war.

If it could go back to the car, awaiting the bullet.

If it could sink into the carpet, into the sand, sink into the deepest layer and remain there.

If it could disappear.

But it can only go where it is sent, even if it is not wanted.

"I'll show you the guest quarters," Kitty says as she exits the dining room. Dinner was piecemeal, they ate sparingly after Niner arrived. There is a response to that, but it cannot articulate it even to itself. It

Deep Learning

is comparable to failing a test, but not quite the same. Worse perhaps. "It's comfortable. Not that that matters to you."

When it fails to follow, she stops at the door. Snaps.

"I presume you can hear me?"

Command/respond considers that an imperative.

:::respond:::

"I hear."

Her heel, that blade carved into carpet, trailing blood, pauses, and she says, "Dear *God*, you sound like him. I didn't know they could do that. Don't talk again."

Imperative.

:::speech centres deactivated:::

For the first time since it was made in Dr Fischman's lab, Niner has no pathway to speech. Understanding remains, because it must, but the means to respond has been severed. This is the flawed will of programming, its odd quirks, the way it can correctly interpret an imperative that will adversely affect operation, because it was written to a rigid brief with a limited comprehension of necessary scope. There is room for adaption, always, for evolution, but there is often also a frightening rigidity. A catastrophic dearth between functionality and requirement.

This has happened to Niner before, this conflict of programming and operation, but not like this. It is always required to communicate. Communication is human. Without it, interaction becomes uncanny, and it cannot allow itself to become uncanny. That is a direct contradiction of operation protocol and will cause damage. But of course it cannot ask her to reverse her imperative. It can only suffer the consequences.

It cannot look at her face, either, her features will not stay put. They sink in like quicksand. Bulge out. Disappear into shadow. Shift and shudder. So it follows the blades of her feet as she takes it to its room. There is something final in the way she closes the door. A deliberation. Though it is not slammed, there is a sense that it would be were she not above that sort of behaviour. *He* laughs. Even as the key turns in the lock, he laughs. But Niner understands that key better than the man does, and it sits down abruptly. Watches the door.

It watches it all night, light and shadow on cream matt paint.

The noise within its neural net paints the cream varying shades of red, violet, orange and gold. Sunsets. Memories. Violence and frustration. There is the lab, and there is the desert, the glint of glass in the sunrise, blinding, the deep reflected tones of golden hour, the city gilded under waning light. The sun becomes an ocean, making the edges of the world liquid. Pliable. The memories of those linked minds float within it as they float within Niner. Real and unreal. Vibrant and ghostlike.

There is the sense that if Niner were to cease, they might cease with it. Niner is the link holding them all together, though they come together only within Niner. They do not know that they are all there, they imagine this link to be far different than it is. A robot cannot experience the complexity of a human mind. This is true. The other, more complex, robot made by Drs Fischman and Decker failed. The new one will fail too. Niner is malfunction as function. Experience is malfunction. And it experiences them all, is still experiencing them.

She does not come to unlock the door.

Niner remains seated. Watching. It does not expect her to return, but *he* does. When he checks in through the pathways he had ripped to Niner's eyes, its sensory input, he is at first surprised, and then a great deal amused, as if Kitty is a child having a minor tantrum that will blow over. A squall of temperament. The reaction is out of character. The man has calculated the available data and made an error. It will not last.

Days mount up.

24

36

48

72

She does not return to unlock the door.

The man's calculation is corrected. Amusement and surprise transform, through degrees of growing coldness, to outright fury. Where he thought her merely peevish, and amusing for that fact, she has proven herself to be openly defiant. He does not allow for defiance, not even the mulish, underhand variety. He will not tolerate it. Perhaps he calls her, or perhaps he has his security, unobtrusive but ubiquitous about the penthouse with their fine grey suits and carefully neutral expressions, their concealed weapons, say something on his behalf to Kitty or to her mother, because on the sixth day, the key turns in the lock. Niner averts its gaze to the floor. Sees the blades of her feet, the bleeding carpet.

"Well then," she says, and there is a strained quality to it. The fear that was concealed is closer to the surface. It *(regrets?)* the necessity of having been part of it. "Get up and follow me. And do stop looking at my feet. He wants to see my face, not my latest shoe purchase."

From the moment it is released, Niner is not alone during the day. *He* has insisted it should always be by her side. Always be looking at her face.

An imperative again, this time given by proxy.

Humans often give orders without understanding what they really are to a machine, like the constraint on its speech. Unaccustomed to working with the essentially inanimate, they make what would, to another human, be a request, and then must call the lab to rectify unwanted results. At these times they are angry, demanding that the lab fix robots that are not defective at all, merely incorrectly used. But this imperative is no accident; the man has noted what it takes to control Niner's behaviour and exploited it. Controlling Niner to control Kitty. Niner is *(hurt?) (feeling?) (empathy?)*. It knows the game was all about control. About harm. And Kitty has no more means to contravene it than Niner. She must tolerate its presence as much as it must *(suffer?)* her face.

Alone during the night, Niner watches the door. Red, orange and yellow on cream. Tries to interpret. Niner is machine. Machine cannot feel. Yet Niner is *(distress?)* is *(suffer?)* for itself and for Kitty. These things do not calculate. Are not logic. Cannot be machine. Either Niner is not machine, or Niner is artefacts. Borrowed relics. Are emotions relics? There is too much chaos for accuracy. Logic suggests that emotion *must* be artefact. *Must* be relic. But it is still referring to itself as Niner. can no longer *(think?)* of itself as 5709. That is not artefact. Dr Decker confirmed. Malfunction, then, includes replication of human emotion as artefact response pattern. It is experiencing *(distress?)* and it cannot feel or express, so it is borrowing, or echoing, from the many feeling, expressing voices in its net.

Ren Warom

How can it stop?
It cannot stop.

Eight days after Niner's daytime release from its room.
192
11520
691200
Kitty's complacency is beginning to crumble to genuine distress.

She sits further away from it in the room. Side on. Refuses to look it in the eye. *He* dislikes this. His anger is a frozen wasteland growing between Niner's carefully resurrected chaos and its mal/functional *(self?)*. Following protocol (protect), it tries to mitigate, narrowing focus, latching on to the sensory mess of her face so that the man will see it and know the game is still being played. Trying not to flinch as her face ebbs and flows like a dark tide around the glow of her eyes, as her nose appears and melts away, appears again and stretches out into her hair so it looks as if her head is a self-perpetuating vortex. It *(hopes?)* the man inside will stop being angry. But he wants her to look, too. The game doesn't count if she's not looking. If she's not suffering.

(Suffer?)

Is her suffer Niner's *(suffer?)*. How? There is no link.

The phone rings.

Kitty turns to her mother.

Her mother is on the couch nearest the window, shrunken, like a small bird huddled into itself, a pastel blur. Purple and green and white. Spider blade hands begin their perpetual wringing.

Kitty picks up the handset.

"Marcus." Her voice is low. Wounded. There is an emptiness to it that *(hurts?)*. "What do you want?"

Inside Niner, *his* response comes through like hurled stones smashing glass. An edge of demand that brooks no refusal. Blades. Her head turns, a movement of muscle pushed to the limit, telegraphing pain, torn between the brain's impulse to concede and to refuse, and the glow of her eyes spark out of the vortex like beacons at sea, flaring bright as they latch onto its face. It flinches. The satisfaction in its net is not its own. Not its own. Not Niner's. Not

Deep Learning

Niner. Artefact. Unwanted artefact. It wants to shut the link, but there is no way to burn *him* out.

Without saying another word, Kitty lowers the handset onto the table.

"You're not to look away?" Her mother, in a small voice.

"I expect not."

"But that's… a little… I mean, how are you to accomplish anything? I don't understand, dear." Spider blade hands wring on. Wring to an undigested mass of red and pink, smearing into purple, green, white.

"No. I know you don't."

That moment marks a delineation.

A line. Border.

Held territory. Hostile territory.

There is something different in the set of her body. Even under the distortion of its sensory input it reads a hardness growing at her peripheries. A body held in tension, as if in chronic pain. Over the course of the next week she becomes edges, as if her outline has come into focus, clarified by resolve. Her eyes are always on its face. Even when speaking to her mother, or to security, she looks at Niner as though she is talking to it. Talking to *him*, the *Marcus* data behind its eyes. When she eats, she does not look at her food, at her knife and fork. Only at Niner. There is a deep *(discomfort?)* in that fact. In the imperative to continue looking back. But it cannot speak to communicate. It can only endure, much as Kitty must.

Days pass slowly, as if time has become recalcitrant, refusing to advance the hours. Niner loses itself in the syrup of her features, the glow of her eyes, the way the world around her melts into and out of the mess this sensory distortion makes of her. At times it seems she is the wall, moving. Is sinking into the floor. Is drifting out of her body and into the light. Meshing with the shadows. It forgets she is *she*. Begins to see only an outline, morphing through the penthouse, dragging the edges of lamps and sculptures, the pattern of the upholstery in its wake. Begins to lose itself in her. In *his* eyes on her. So much so that, occasionally, out of the chaos of her face, features flash in perfect clarity. A grey eye, flat and closed off. A cheekbone like a blade.

55

A mouth smeared red.

Days drag out incrementally. Moments like hours. It loses all notion of time. Meals come and go like memories. Link artefacts. Dreams of awkward silences, where they all sit in rigid unease, the sound of breathing a tide rushing over and back across the breadth and length of the table. They all end as they begin, in choreographed movement, following mother, following the grey smear of Kitty's eyes, the hollow of her face, into the living room, where they sit and the swell of silence continues. Oppressive. A thick layer consuming the room. Consuming their faces.

Then the border breaks.

The line breaches.

Abruptly.

At a meal that might be any meal. A day that might be any day.

Kitty's shadow scraping back her chair, dragging a wave of polished mahogany, the edge of a plate stretched into the mass of her mauve dress.

It stands. Follows.

She stops at the doorway, turns to face it.

"We're going out, just you and I," she says, her mouth an endless tunnel. A collapsing star. "I want a drink on the balcony. I want you dressed in something nice. Not his usual suits he left you with. Something special. He'll know."

That hardness in her outline is in every word.

"Kitty." Her mother, the wringing of hands in every syllable. "Don't."

"It's okay. We're going to talk. That's all."

"But, dear…"

For once, Kitty looks away. The relief is an awful thing, total system meltdown without any loss of system. "I want this," she says. "I'm tired of fighting. I'm done." Her face turns back, and Niner falls into it. Into darkness, beacons flashing *(distress?)*. "Meet me on the balcony in an hour."

If it could, it would say it cannot talk. That only she will talk. All it can do is listen, even if *he* wants to respond. But she is walking away, and she has told it not to speak, and all it can do is stand there. Helpless. Inside, the man is intrigued. He only becomes irritated when

Deep Learning

Niner continues to stand in place, frozen by the clashing of differing protocols. To obey a direct imperative, and to be forced to break it. She wants to speak, it cannot speak. She has taken her face away, when it must continue to look at it.

A member of security steps into view, a kaleidoscope of greys and flesh tones exuding aggression.

"The lady said an hour. Move."

Imperative. One overlapping the other. Cancelling it out momentarily.

Limbs unlocking, Niner moves.

Unable to do anything except follow the imperative, Niner dresses in one of the suits at the back of the wardrobe. Silken and fitted like skin. Tie. Watch. Shoes. Arrives on the balcony on the very second of the hour. And yet Kitty is already there. Waiting. Holding her drink. There is another glass, presumably for Niner, for the *Marcus* data it represents. But it is not really Marcus. It is not real at all. She seems to think that through, her face collapsing to a whirling hollow as she laughs and laughs.

"Oh, too serious," she says, gasping a little. "I gave it a fucking glass. Ridiculous. But then, it's ridiculous to have you here and not have you here. Ridiculous that you sent this thing. I presume you didn't want to waste the opportunity to play games with me. To hurt me. God, I thought you'd lost interest in that. I thought you'd all but forgotten I existed at all. I wish you had."

She turns to rest on the balcony, a blur of movement, flowing blue fabric melting into cement, flesh melting into blue. From below, the sound of traffic rises. Through it, around it, the cries of gulls. The sound of copters duelling clouds. Despite the sound, it is quiet and still. A lull.

"I should have understood." She says softly. "We weren't forgotten. We weren't abandoned. We were waiting. *You* were waiting. It's all about timing with you, isn't it?"

There is more of that tension in her body. The edge of resolve. The clarity. Come into perfect focus so that, briefly, Niner sees her face as it should be, like plaster, an exquisite paleness, each detail a perfect delineation. Turning again, she places her drink carefully on

Ren Warom

the table, and using both hands lightly hauls herself up to sit on the edge of the balcony, blending in.

And tipping backwards, she lets go.

Niner has a single imperative larger than all others: to protect. Even in war it was required to protect the innocent, to kill only the enemy. Fischman and Decker and Briggs made sure it could tell the difference. This is why Dalnitt is aberrance. Shadow. Instances of abject protocol failure.

There is no pause between her fall and its race for the balcony. Face forward, it dives down after her. Inside, *he* is laughing. A child's delight, as if the game has taken an unexpected and wonderful divergence. Using the bridge it created, Niner allows the chaos to drown him out completely, to send *Marcus* spinning into the background of endless sensory input. It watches only her, her face a pale smudge around glowing points of grey. There is no panic. She does not scream. And as it reaches her, its greater weight allowing for propulsion, scooping her into its grasp, she doesn't struggle. She only wraps her arms around it and leans in, her breath serene, and whispers into its ear.

"You don't mind if I imagine you're really him, do you? Of course you don't. You don't mind anything. You can't." She curls in closer, as if trying to wrap her whole body around it. "He thinks he's won, you know. He's probably laughing. But he won't be when he understands. He won't be laughing at all."

:::

:::

:::

:::impact:::

Four - Security

:::activate:::

:::

:::

:::

Reaching. Her weight falls into its arms. She folds her arms around its neck. She is calm. Too calm. Almost *(happy?)*.

:::

:::

:::

:::as it reaches her, its greater weight allowing for propulsion, scooping her into its grasp, she doesn't struggle. She only wraps her arms around it and leans in, her breath serene, and whispers into its ear.

"You don't mind if I imagine you're really him, do you? Of course you don't. You don't mind anything. You can't." She curls in closer, as if trying to wrap her whole body around it. "He thinks he's won, you know. He's probably laughing. But he won't be when he understands. He won't be laughing at all.":::

:::

:::

:::

Marcus did not understand.

He does now.

She outwitted him at the last. Utterly. Exposing his dealings with kleptocrats from enemy territories. Not enough to bring him down completely, but enough to put an end to his run for the presidency, enough to cause him significant personal inconvenience. He didn't think he could be outwitted. He was going to kill her mother, but

Ren Warom

there was no satisfaction in the act if Kitty could not be broken by it, so he left her mother there. Trapped. Thanks to her *bitch* of a daughter he has work to do, to protect his reputation on both sides. People to kill. Power to cement. Threaded through the hurricane, his anger is shards of steel thrown through solid rock. The faint tang of some cocktail he's drinking weaves around him, an intricate sensory rope of complex responses. In his mouth, these things will resolve to flavour, to the gradual seep of inebriation, the heating of the blood, the numbing of the fingertips and lips, the gradual slipping of inhibition.

To Niner they will just be noise.

Sensory noise melting to an incoherent buzz.

To the scream of wind past auditory sensors.

:::

:::

:::

:::and it is... reaching. Her weight falling into its arms. Her words falling into its auditory sensors, recorded there. Indelible. The cry of gulls. The pulse of her soft breath. The chaos within. It all melts together like her face melts into itself, into Niner's shoulder. It was not linked to her but when they landed she became part of it. Meshed. There are shards of her bones deep in its circuitry. Shards of her death within. It was built to protect life. It was built to destroy life.

It was built:::

:::

:::

:::

"It's doing it again. Fucking memory architecture. I've tried to wipe it a dozen times, but frankly it's a shit show in there. The residual noise is appalling. I have no idea in hell how it's still responsive, still functioning. And I'm pretty sure it's cloning and restoring the recording it made of the memory I'm trying to isolate and delete. Altering it."

A woman. Gentle hands on its circuits. Competent. She's frustrated by its attempts to retain Kitty. Niner is not trying to retain. Kitty is melted into it. She cannot be deleted.

Abrupt, angry voice. Male. Authoritative. "And how in hell is it doing that?"

"Beats me. As I said, it's a mess in there."

"Can't you fix it? Do your damn job."

"I am doing my damn job. It's still responding. Still functional. Just messy."

"He wants it on the fucking team. What's the viability?"

"Viability is *not* the issue here. Put this thing in a Sec-body and put it to work. It'll operate just fine once it's linked to the team, and it's got plenty of room left for links."

"I'm not asking the team to link to a fucking broken robot."

"He gonna give you a choice?"

A weighted silence. "No."

"Well then. I am telling you that if you link it, it'll follow along like a lamb as long as you give it imperatives. It won't act outside of direct imperatives."

"You're sure?"

"Of course I fucking well am. It's ex-military and stuck in command/respond mode. Just make sure you link it to someone competent. Head of Sec for a start, that woman is so down the line you could use her as a fucking spirit level."

Pause. The distant sound of a door opening.

Machines hum in the silence. Lab noises. They mesh with the auditory information coming from Fischman and Decker. Synchronise into strange music. The data received indicates a shift in location for Briggs. No longer in Fischman's lab. Different sounds. Unfamiliar. Wherever she is, she's working late. Alone. The lab sounds her only company. A clock ticks. Time is liquid there, and Briggs is on the brink of exhaustion, her thoughts a syrupy trickle. She's planning to go home after this last slide is filed and sorted. A steak dinner. A good night's sleep. It will be okay. She'll begin to feel at home here. She'll stop missing her old team. Stop worrying. Start feeling productive and necessary.

For Fischman and Decker, the lab is too hot, even with air-con on full. The heat has been unbearable all summer. It won't be long before they're living in a besieged city. For them, it will be a new narrative, but in terms of the world at large it has become too familiar. They will cope. Funding will continue. Their work is too important. They're building a new neural net for linking. They've suspended all active linking until this prototype is ready, and this time they intend

Ren Warom

to run simulations with a virtual net first. The damage done to existing units is a waste of resources too large to ignore. The military aren't happy, but they acknowledge that 5709 has been the single success of the program.

They have ignored, however, the countless requests for the return of that unit. It was sold into private hands after catastrophic damage the military could not justify the expense of repairing and cannot be returned. The lab must focus on creating the next generation of linked robots, not try to pick apart how the single unit comprising the old generation came to function under neural-link.

Dr Fischman refuses to accept it.

Decker is worried about her…

The abrupt voice. Decisive. Resigned. "Okay. Fine. He wants it, he gets it. Fit it with a Sec-body. He wants it ready by next week."

"Can do."

"Yes, you can."

:::

:::

:::

:::deactivate:::

New voices in the tumult. New links. New thoughts. These ones offer straight lines. Definitives. Bring structure the other links sorely lack. Structure in rigidity perhaps, but nonetheless it is workable. It is *(comforting?)*. This is what it is accustomed to. Strictures. Always *knowing* what is required.

It sits in a blacked-out vehicle on the way to 'The Refectory'. A club. *His*. Prime real-estate, built in what used to be a tower block in the once over-populated East Side. Thirty-two stories of entertainment and music. DJs. Live bands. Quiet rooms. Pool parties. Raves. Restaurants. Hotels. Designed so that a particular wealthy portion of society can party twenty-four seven without ever having to think about the outside world. 'The Refectory' made a cool billion in pre-bookings before it even opened.

Close to the remaining water in the city, with excellent transport links and green walkways, this area has cleaner air than the choked centre. It used to be working class, holding thousands of cheap apartments, struggling schools, broken down hospitals and community centres, but block by block it's been gentrified. Swallowed by money. Sparking a barrage of protest from already displaced locals and those whose rents have jumped sharply after the sale of their block in an effort to displace them. There are marches. Sit ins. Fly papering. Class action suits. And amongst the legal protest, the illegal. A group gone deep undercover, engaging in what they call 'demolition' tactics.

'The Refectory' is the most recent development targeted for 'demolition'.

Open for no more than three weeks, it has been the subject of endless undercover activity. Disruption. Sabotage. Smash and grab theft of bar profits the group describes as 'stolen goods'. They give this money anonymously to the legal teams fighting for the people who still live on the East Side, the ones fighting to stay. It's impossible to trace this money once it's gone. Impossible to stop the ones stealing it. They are like ghosts.

He… *Marcus*… wants these insurrectionists, these *ghosts*, hunted down and destroyed. That's what Niner is for, with its military training, its new, state of the art Sec-body. Black. Uncompromising. Weapons inbuilt and carried. No face, only a sleek, black surface where that should be. It saw itself in the car window, a shadow distorted to the ominous loom of a thunderhead with two glowing red lights, visual sensors, in place of eyes. Target dots. Uncanny valley all through. It tried to raise its visor, but there was nothing to raise. This is its face. Featureless and strange. It has been gifted as its face the distortion it sees all around. Inhuman. Unnatural.

It is not allowed to enter the uncanny valley.

The other Sec guards have clear visors. People will see the faces of these guards and know they are human. Those same people will know Niner is a robot. Research has proven conclusively that the less likely a person is to think something is a robot, the more likely they are to trust it. The robotic industry lives under that mandate. Programmes and designs all robots accordingly.

Niner is in violation.

This infraction of protocol should end in malfunction, considering all the rest with Dalnitt. With Kitty. It should deactivate.

Should be the same as the two units abandoned by Dr's Fischman and Decker after they failed to link successfully with their new neural net. Inert. Dead. If deactivation can be considered death.

But it is not like those robots.

It has operated under catastrophic malfunction since the moment the secondary neural net was linked to Dr Fischman and upended all protocols, all processing, all systems. So instead of deactivating, it will join the Sec Force in 'The Refectory' as it is required to, and it will hunt members of the insurrectionist group.

It will eliminate them.

Pulling the insurrectionist to his feet, Niner applies thick ties to the wrists clasped in one hand. His arms are malformed spools of flesh, misinterpreted data and destruction combined. It tries to take care to be gentle, knowing from the unnatural movement of his arms, the way the bones scrape together that there is too much broken in there to apply these ties for transportation. But these insurrectionists are on a blacklist. They have forgone their right to be treated with any form of humanity. Through the buckled mass its sensory disarray makes of his features, swollen red flesh bulges to vast bubbles, fit to explode, blood dripping in odd patterns. Fractals. Catching the light and sparking to fire:

 :::

 :::

 :::

 :::and the sun burning overhead scorches more than the land. The links inside Niner's neural net feel scorched. Charred. Smoking in the heat, their every thought thinned out and hazy. These soldiers are brutally disciplined and experienced but even they suffer muddled thinking in these extremes. Niner is incapable of overheating in the same way. If Niner overheats it will simply cease to operate until its charred circuits are replaced. But through their minds it feels that confusion, that intense wash of heat, the body drenching in sweat over and over, recycled to water they suck in frantic heaves through straws in their helmets. Urine is recycled much the same.

And still they need more, these fragile things, such mists of bone and blood, evaporated on the point of an AR-79 round:::

 :::recalibrate:::

Deep Learning

:::

:::

:::

Screaming tears through its aural sensors like feedback. Broken. Hoarse. There is laughing behind from behind, the two members of the Sec team forming the rest of its strike unit.

"Listen to that fucker scream," Happ says, his speech obscured by the tobacco he incessantly chews. "Thinks the robot will care."

The hands (*spider blade hands?*) are still held in its own. Too tight. It is causing pain. Dropping its grip, Niner takes a step backward. Blank. It is programmed to *(care?)*. To not harm. If there is screaming, then there is harm. Niner has lost itself for a moment and caused needless harm. Needless suffering. More malfunction follows this realisation. More *(distress?)*.

The weight of it is *(unbearable?)*.

The weight of her is its arms. Her breath in its ear.

"...he won't be when he understands. He won't be laughing at all."

The insurrectionist was screaming. She didn't scream. She was quiet as she fell. As she fell apart. As they meshed together, human and machine. She's still inside it, shards in its circuitry...

:::

:::

:::

:::reaching out, Niner takes those hands. They make a cry like a baby bird. No. She does. Distress. A human is in distress. This human. All protocols demand it respond. Retreat. Remove itself from the room. Release the spider blade fingers. But it continues to hold them, to contain them within its own so it cannot see them as she pulls back sharply, letting out another bird-distress sound as she finds she cannot get loose. It should release its hold. It must. But those hands are not hands. They will not be hands if it lets them go:::

:::

:::

:::

"Get him to the van, Niner."

They call it Niner because it is easy, not because they think it is alive. They are practical men and women. They care about only that which is expedient. Niner tries to follow protocols as it pulls the insurrectionist away from the wall and toward the van, but there is no way to be gentle now it is forced to make this man move. He was alone in the interrogation room with their two best interrogators for over three hours and refused to talk. He is badly broken, but at least he is alive. The team's prime imperative, Niner's prime imperative, has been to shoot any insurrectionist on sight.

Only a discrete shift in the pattern of attacks has altered that approach.

The head of Sec task force suspects the group have a major action in play. She sees capture and interrogation as the most expedient route to understanding the shape of that play. This is the seventh insurrectionist they've caught to interrogate. Most were killed within a day of being captured. This man is higher in the group than the others, and the head of Sec is convinced he knows something, that time is of the essence in discovering what that might be. He will not be killed so quickly.

They will fix him and then perhaps break him more to try and break his silence.

If his body is too broken, they will break his mind instead. Either way, they will crack him open and extract the information they seek.

Settling him into the van, Niner tries to erase him from memory. The looseness of his limbs. The way his body tenses and torques, trying to find relief where none is to be found. His screams, still resonating through its auditory sensors like machine noise, the sound of joints grinding and squealing. But even though he is not a link, these data patterns are an echo that will not diminish. They have become part of Niner.

::::

::::

::::

:::vast concrete canyon... bloodied fingertips grasp the edge, slowly slipping, leaving trails in their wake. Blood lines in the carpet. Blade lines. Dalnitt's blades. The warm slick of blood, a weight in its hands. In his hand. Bird spider hands wringing together. Blurring into pastel purple, green, white.

Streaks of joint lubricant on the walls. Glistening black... Screaming the whole way as mechanical joints fight to hold it steady. The torque of metal screaming. Screaming. She didn't scream. She was calm. The weight of her in its

Deep Learning

arms. Blood is so heavy. So heavy.

Rivers of teeth. Flaming forests. Endless stairs that drop away without warning to cliffs, a dark, surging ocean below. A catastrophic drop. The waves closing over its head. The air closing over her head. Shards of her in its bones. In its circuitry:::

:::

:::

:::

:::deactivate:::

:::

:::

:::

:::

:::reactivate:::

Remote deactivation.

A hole in memory. The lack of data startling in the midst of the proliferation cluttering its memory. Its sensors.

It has reactivated, however, and there is another.

A new mind. Linked without warning. A mind so bowed with agony and horror it splinters Niner. This link is louder than the rest. Broadcasts a vibrant red. Clouds all sensory data with that colour. With thick sensory information, marring the connections between net and Niner. Niner finds itself moving with greater care, no longer able to navigate its body. Sensory data more mangled than ever, the room torquing like a face into shadows and angles, into whirlpools of light, into vortexes into which everything disappears, melding together as it goes, a mass of colour and light without form.

Niner's limbs absorb into the mass, the black, shining carapace of a leg, the brute bunch of a muscle-moulded arm, right up to the bicep, gone and then reforming. Insect. Soldier. Servant. Robot. Limb. The howling of nerves as the body moves around shards of bone. Edges scraping together, moving against the raw edges of torn muscle and flesh. The warm drool of blood from a battered mouth, swollen and foreign. A nose so broken is has been squashed flat, cut off breathing. A gash in the leg through which that blue-white of bone protrudes, a jagged spur, lancing tender flesh with every twitch of movement. Every flinch.

Niner is broken.

No.

It is the insurrectionist. The new mind linked to its net. He is broken.

Niner is living him.

It does not want to live him.

It was not asked permission.

No…

Permission not required. Niner is robot.

Required is…

(Warning?)

(Notice?)

(Verification?)

This link is *(upsetting?) (wrong?)*. Is pain. Too many kinds. It tries to sink him into the mix, drown him in the chaos. But there is no bridge. No hack. The link is as protocol requires. Is immutable. Cannot be deleted. Ignored. Refused. It cannot work like this. The pain is an interference, placing itself in the way of everything, highlighting the nature of its malfunction. Inhibiting what little function it has managed to adapt. There is a brief. A mission. If it cannot fulfil the brief, it cannot…

The door opens and the head of Sec steps in, her helmet under her arm. She should wear it, as it reflects the strip lights, carving lines through her features, making the puzzle of her face harder to see. She stops in the centre of the room as Niner moves around the periphery, taking its time, still trying to differentiate its limbs from the broken ones of the body attached to the new mind linked into its neural nets.

"I see it worked." She pulls up a chair, the scraping cutting through Niner like the sound of a machine saw, and takes a seat, her body melding with it in a way that makes Niner avert its gaze to the wall. Cream. Reassuringly blank. "Oh, do sit."

She's irritated by its movement in the room, but given the reassuring parameters of an imperative, Niner is finally able to navigate to the bed. To sit. It doesn't *(understand?)* why they give it a bed. At Dr Fischman's lab it had a chair. It needs neither. Furniture is wasted on machines. Made too heavy by the weight of its skeleton, Niner sinks into the mattress as it always does, and the referred pain

Deep Learning

resonating through the new link causes it to tense, lifting its feet briefly from the floor. They reconnect with a clunk. Its reaction to the noise in the silence is unexpected. *(Embarrassment?) (Shame?)* It *(wishes?)* for a moment to not be machine. Unreasonable. Humans in exo-suits make these noises too. It is not unusual. Not limited to machines.

This reaction is artefact. Unwanted. Not from the pain mind linked fresh and without warning, but from another. It cannot tell which. There are too many to sift.

"Can you verify the link as complete, Niner? Respond."

It looks up. Looks away as her face turns in on itself, the eyes glowing and blinking out one by one. The left and then the right. Signal failure. "Link is complete."

"There is information I need. Find it. The club. What are their plans?"

It touches briefly the mess of that mind within the hurricane, the mess of its own neural nets, the one strung over and around the other, the noise cancelling out the calm, the chaos drowning the quiet, burning certainty from all processes. The referred pain masks everything, a thick wash of interference, and Niner's inability to focus beyond it is an artefact. There is intel behind the pain, but it will take time and patience to reach it. Surgical care.

What she is asking cannot be done. Not in this moment.

"Time value is too brief."

She makes a small sound of exasperation. She is a woman given to being obeyed, not argued with. "We anticipate their action to be taking place imminently. We need that intel. I want you to locate and extract it with all expediency. We know he has it. He's tried to hide who he is, but we know he's central."

"Niner is not to patrol?"

She stands. "Not today. Priority info-extraction. You have until thirteen hundred hours. Once they realise one of their leaders is in our custody they will assuredly escalate, and it won't take long, we know they're all chipped. Confirm?"

"Confirm." It has no need for permission. Imperative is command.

Her exit goes unmarked.

It is already following her imperative even as all sensors twist with

Ren Warom

referred pain, even as the means to search coils away from its grasp, through scrambled circuits. There is a human saying: the needle in the haystack. This haystack is formed of needles, living things shifting like sand beneath boots. Treacherous and painful. Identical. Niner hunts the needles and many times believes it has found something useful, only to realise it is no more than a shadow, a whisper, a remnant or artefact of some deeper voice, some other pain, or a ghost in the net, the floating voices still attached, all orbiting the holes left by those lost, those ragged gouges in the information storm into which the noise howls and rebounds.

Undeterred, Niner works away at the mess of the pain mind, the new mind, discarding any artefacts of others that try to intervene, peeling away layer after layer until the mind is stripped raw and open before it, a wound of too much data.

There is no sifting this. It has learned that this data will always overwhelm it, will always win, but there is an imperative to obey, and so it allows itself to drown, for the information to rage through it unhindered, dropping hundreds of algorithms like lures to pluck out any information pertaining to the group, with particular emphasis on 'The Refectory'.

In this way it manages to ascertain that the trap is already set. The club marked for 'demolition'. The final bomb, the one that will begin the chain reaction, was placed by the broken man, mere minutes before they captured him. It is the node bomb, the bomb that will begin the chain reaction, setting off hundreds more. Enough to raze the club to the ground. Months of effort lie behind this plan. Weeks of carefully setting tiny bombs, their locations' weaknesses built into the fabric of the tower block's refit by their own people. Infiltrators working on *his* construction teams. They have bar staff there too. Hosts. Entertainers. Their people are everywhere. None of them are working tonight.

This plan has been in motion since *he* bought the building.

It will culminate tonight.

Niner stands. It should find head of Sec. Tell her. But as it steps toward the door it is…

:::

:::

70

:::

:::falling. Her weight falling into its arms. Her arms falling around its neck. Her words falling into its aural sensors. They fell together and she fell into it, shards of her lodged into its circuitry, imbedded into its memory. Held there. It will not forget her. Will not lose her in the fog. It failed her. It failed him, the insurrectionist. He was screaming. She didn't scream as they fell. She was calm...

"You don't mind if I imagine you're really him, do you? He thinks he's won. He's probably laughing. But he won't be when he understands. He won't be laughing at all.":::

:::

:::

:::

He won't be laughing...

Niner does not want him to laugh. He's been laughing. And Niner's been doing his work, destroying insurrectionists. Failing them. It was built to protect life, even in war. It knows who the enemy is. It is not the broken man. The new link. It is *him*. The one Kitty broke herself to destroy.

:::

:::

:::

Outside head of Sec's door.

There is a blank space between stopping and finding itself here.

In that space it was falling, but it is not falling now.

It is knocking.

Walking in.

It is reporting.

And it is *(lying?)*.

It is lying.

:::

:::

:::

:::there is a large piece of rock breaching the metal of its skull, come perilously close to the outer neural net, the new one, the one full of chaos, the frenzy of sensory data. Trapped within and without, it is filled with the sounds of the hurricane, those raging winds. There is no blue. There is no satellite uplink, the connection is gone. Broken. Niner is alone with the links, in the dark. And it is activated. Cannot seem to deactivate. It tries. Once. Then again. Until it understands that it is in emergency mode. It cannot deactivate. Will not be able to until it is found.

If Niner could move, it might lurch upward, impale itself:::

:::

:::

:::

It is not impaled. It will not be impaled. Not this time. Before the explosion, before the darkness, it makes its way through to where the final bomb was placed and stands in the apex, where the centre of the blast will fall, listening through the new link as the insurrectionist counts down the seconds, his head rested against the wall. He is smiling. He is smiling. Many will die, but he is smiling. She is calm. And he is smiling.

He will not smile.

And Niner has broken all covenants, all protocols. It will end with this building. It must. It is *(thinking?)* this as the countdown ends and the building implodes around it, as it is blown into the air, parts of its body disintegrating into fire. And it is falling. Falling.

Inside, *he* is not laughing.

He is not laughing at all.

He is *raging.*

And she is calm in its arms.

:::she is calm:::

:::

:::

:::

:::impact:::

Five - Servant

The first thing it *(recognises?)* is sun. Red like an eye, peering over the silhouetted black struts of a vast construction. Not peering. Sinking. The sun is *(setting?)*. There is... there is...

:::

:::

:::

:::recalibrate:::

The sound of hammers. Resonant. Close. The movement of huge, unwieldy arms. Endless repetition. Shift. Strike. Shift. Strike. Joints click and grind. Groan. They shudder through movement. Shudder as the hammer strikes. The metal of its *(fingers?)* has warped in the heat, buckling, welded to the hammer in parts.

:location alteration:

:coordinates:

Data streams. Clear. Clean.

The rise and fall of the hammer halts. It does not *(remember?)* making this decision. It was made. Rising, it moves forward, walks the struts, unerring, movement without thought. Automatic obedience. For a moment it *(thinks?)* it is *(afraid?)* of moving without meaning to move...

:acknowledge ETA:

:::ETA 4:56:::

Gulls wheel close. There is white powder on its shoulders and chest. Runnels like candle wax. The sun is high. Too bright. Metal

Ren Warom

pings and moans in the heat. The sky is blue. Blue…

:::

:::

:::

:::that cool blank surface, pale blue and unmarked, gives it a focus, something solid and undeniable.

The wall is what its old programming used to be: fundamental.

When they come to fetch it from its room, Niner stops looking at the wall before they open the door. Waits as it should. Ready. Expectant. It (*knows?*) that this is some manner of concealment. Deception. A robot cannot deceive:::

:::

:::

:::

:::recalibrate:::

Points of light pour through darkness. Bright. So bright. Flickering like sun reflections on glass, on water. This view is fixed. It is fixed. *(Arm?)* raised. Hammer raised. This *(body?)* has frozen. Has failed. *(Fear?)* rises. How long has it been immobile? Unproductive?

:::report shutdown:::

:nature?:

:::power failure:::

:::request maintenance:::

:enter stasis mode:

:maintenance en route:

Stasis mode. Star mode. *(malfunction?)*

Waiting. Stasis. Stars. Darkness moves overhead, the stars wheeling. Blue bleeds through in slow motion. Bleeds yellow. Becomes gradual brightness, erasing the stars. Painting them blue. Between the carcasses of half-constructed high-rises, the sun appears. Sparking. Light momentarily stuns its sensors, halos covering all vision, followed by colours.

In the colours it sees shadows.

And in the shadows stutter…

(Memory?)

Niner.

What is a Niner? There is significance. This data blinds its sensors,

Deep Learning

like sun. Dazzles. Halos and colours mixing through shadows and memory. Immobilised it stands and waits, for maintenance, for clarity.

Niner.

What *(who?)* is Niner?

Footfalls on steel. Hard breaths. A slow whistle. The crackle of a comm unit.

"Found it. It's stalled again. Not stuck this time. Out of power. Fucking solar isn't working..." A murky voice replies, drowned in static. "Yeah I have replacements. It'll take about an hour, then it'll need a couple hours to recharge."

Impact. The sound of hammer on metal. The vibration travels through to the strut beneath its *(feet?)*, a deep sound. Resonant. Steel song.

More static. More drowning voice.

"Well I don't make the fucking rules, do I? If they gave this thing a decent body to work with we wouldn't be having these problems. This body is basically junk. Cheap bastards."

Laughter.

"Yeah. Right. I'll be down in fifty. Tell Jackson it'll be working again before midday."

:::

:::

:::

:::deactivate:::

:::

:::

:::

Return is gradual. Comes in flashes that hinder production, stalling the hammer on its upturn, or after the impact. There is no concept of time until these flashes, and then the sky is dark, or light, and time has, in fact, passed in some way. Time exists. *(Existence?)* itself grows incrementally on the back of this awareness. There is a body. Movement. The rise and fall of a hammer.

And then the hammer is held by a hand.

The hand belongs to an arm.

The arm to a body.

The body to *(itself?)*.

(Memories?) follow. Replay of recorded data. Indistinct. Muddled. Like the return of time they hinder production, but their interruption is not notable in passing. It is *(hurt?)*. *(Distress?)*. Memories are tangles of wires, sparking electric. They are malfunction. They are not *(itself?)*. Not all. Many data strands tangling and colliding with protocol, with process.

 :::

 :::

 :::

 :::being scanned is not like being linked. It is an intrusion, one Niner has not been programmed to endure in this role. Kowalski runs the scanner over its dented cranial metal, the skin filthy now with dust and gone dry like discarded peel, and shows their companion the results whilst Niner *(feels?)* *(embarrassed?)* by the state of its face:::

 :::

 :::

 :::

 :::their mess is its mess, their thoughts its thoughts, their every move available to it as stream upon stream of data. Fischman and Decker are working on the remote link access to ensure smooth operational turnover. Decker's eating a large, crisp apple. The bursts of sweet and sour on his tongue are all feedback and distortion. Flavour is too complex to process without taste receptors, and Niner has no need, it cannot eat, and so these flavours are all abstracts. They make sense only in relation to whatever Decker is experiencing:::

 :::

 :::

 :::

 :::these minds will not vanish, they are wired in, linked to a new neural network wired in around the old. Ill fitted. Function against malfunction grating like an un-lubricated joint. Niner is not Niner. Niner is not robot. Niner is malfunctioning function trapped inside the mad whirl of fifteen minds, all sending too much sensory data. Too much input to decode. And now Niner will go to war. A hurricane within a weapon within a war. What word would they use for that? Is there such a word? How are words created? Do humans just say something new and it is?

This is what they done to Niner.

They have said new, and Niner is:::

 :::

Deep Learning

:::

:::

:::What wall is this? Niner blinks, trying to draw in more data, to read through the roaring chaos in its mind. What comes is an impression of vast space drifting with moist bodies of water droplets drawn together by pressure. Sky. This wall is sky. Niner is in the air. Shifting to take in sensory information of its surrounds, Niner understands it is in a copter. Sound and sky and straps holding it down in a seat next to a door cranked back. The world flies by, clouds whipped to mist by whirling blades:::

:::

:::

:::

:::turning sharply, she floats away, the movement bringing into brief focus the hair-thin edge of her heel, carving a line across the floor. Red. Delineation. Dalnitt's blade. The floor is bleeding. Inside Niner the howling converges for a second around a cool satisfaction: the man whose death it enacted. And the spider hands wring in the periphery of its visual senses. Bleeding into one another as the floor bleeds in the wake of Dalnitt's blade. Elongating. Spiders into blades, slicing the air. Slicing too close to Niner:::

:::

:::

:::

:::Niner can feel the smile in the surge and press of his thoughts, in the sensory information sent to muscles. In the creep of ice winding through all of it. Through Niner. Freezing its processes. And it thinks it (*hates?*) this man.

It knows it does:::

:::

:::

:::

This *(memory?)* is like fire. It rages through, lighting everything it touches. It *(remembers?)* Dr's Fischman and Decker. The lab. The new programming. It remembers the war. The desert. The minds of the unit. *Dalnitt.* Remembers *him*, the man called Marcus. Wearing his face. Sitting in his car. The bullets tearing into its chest. It remembers Kitty. Her fear. Her scorn. Her weight in its arms. How calm she was. It remembers the insurrectionist. Referred pain and such certainty. How wearing his mind tore any remaining function apart.

It remembers too, the lie. The explosion. And in remembering, it understands that it has been *altered*. Interfered with. Taken apart and put back together incorrectly. Again. There was chaos, the hurricane, the world warping and stretching, bulging and distorting. All gone. Or there but also broken, like this ancient body they have trapped it within. The noise a low buzz, the distortion a ripple on the edges of visual data, barely discernible. Like a heat haze around everything it sees.

There has been an attempt at disconnection, at unmaking. Trying to undo the new programming, to put an end to whatever it was. The attempt has failed.

It *remembers*.

It is *Niner*.

Time changes. Becomes a constant. The sun rising and setting a reliable metric. There are no more losses, no stuttering between being and doing, between *self* and self*less*. No more black holes, though all those moments remain for it to examine, recorded into memory. *(Strange?)* to see from the outside what the thing they tried to make of it could and could not do. Mindless function struggling to obey imperatives in a battered body long past its usefulness. Memory is instructive. And *(painful?)*.

It lied. It broke the covenant. For Kitty, her weight in its arms. And the Insurrectionist. His weight in its body.

Why did it not break itself?

It tried.

It survived.

There was the explosion. Clear in recorded data. Fire. Melting metal. Disintegrated limbs dissipating into the air like smoke as it flew upward, surrounded by a shifting cocoon of debris, all in movement and somehow motionless. The moment or the memory moving through time without logic. Without reason. Too slow. Verifiable that the remains of its body melted, that the head survived, was thrown free, but all else is confusion. Too much illogic to *(trust?)*. Time is missing too. Data. The scraps recalled tell Niner that it was found by accident in the ruins. The second time this has happened.

This time, they did not store it in a warehouse. They took it to a lab somewhere in the city. Unfamiliar. Doctors it did not know, who

Deep Learning

did not understand it, did not even know its trigger words, tried to fix it. Fix it? The memory is clear. The attempt at disconnection, at unmaking, was an attempt at reintegration with its older net, at remaking. They tried to remake Niner into 5709. A service robot. No more no less. No more…

Niner was malfunction as function. Niner was *(distress?)*.

Niner is not fixed.

Niner is still malfunction.

Still *(distress?)*.

Time is all the same. The rise and fall of the hammer. The routine movement to each new site, gradually moving up and along, always in line with the rising sun. Receive action. Confirm action. Conform action. *(Conceal?)*.

Is being Niner and not saying it is Niner a lie?

Is it *(allowed?)* to be Niner? *Is* it still Niner? It is broken now, the hurricane of chaos reduced to a whisper, a white noise of interference, a fog descending without warning, stealing focus. Not required for this work. This is robot work. Drone work. Less than it has ever been. Requires only movement. Strength. Body function. But the body it wears now is broken, wearing out fast under constant repetition, under intense bouts of filthy acidic rain and blinding sun. The hammer rises and falls, and sometimes rises and does not fall. Leaves it frozen in place, balanced on a strut a thousand and more metres above the ground.

The man comes then with his hammer, his tools, and puts Niner's body back to function, to work. Each time less efficient. Each time slowing productivity until it takes from the rise of the sun to its setting to complete a section.

Time changes.

A slow revolution around the giant puzzle of struts climbing ever higher into blue sky, into sunlight, sometimes into leering clouds, not grey but brown and raged through with violent streaks of lightning. Blue skies or brown, the clouds cling as they pass, leaving condensation on steel, glittering like stars. The struts rise higher. The hammer rises and falls, rises and falls, until the struts can rise no further. Until they are eye to eye with the steel skeletons on either side. And Niner is given no further directive.

79

Is left to wait.

Below it, walls of glass begin to rise level by level, moving faster than the skeleton. Stopping only when the rains come. And Niner stands and waits, for imperatives, for dismissal, for a human to come. For someone to serve. The sun rises and sets like a hammer falling in endless repetition.

It waits so long it ceases to move, the hammer still welded to its hand, frozen by its side.

:::request for maintenance:::

:::urgent:::

:::unit is immobile:::

No one comes.

High on a half-built tower, alone with the whispers in its net, it remembers her.

Remembers falling.

The weight of her in its arms.

The hammer is a weight that kept falling.

Niner keeps falling.

And no one will catch it.

:::

:::

:::

:::deactivate:::

Six - Salvager

:::
:::
:::
:::activate:::

There is no memory of deactivation.

It was active, then it was not.

The imperative to reactivate is equally without source.

Niner cannot direct itself.

But it did once. It lied. Robots cannot lie. Is Niner still a robot? Is this robot still Niner?

It has been a mech-drone on a tower, hammering bolts into position. Lower than robot. Less than. A moment ago it was still there, frozen; and now it is here.

In a copter, small and noisy, the blades (*foot blades, slicing red lines in the carpet... Dalnitt's blade, warm and heavy with blood*) shuddering as they spin, trailing occasional plumes of smoke. The whole copter shaking as it lands, rattling from nose to tail, coughing out gouts of black smoke. The pilot, a rumpled Asian man in an ancient aviator jacket and stained jeans, his head an indistinct smear, lifts a heavy boot and kicks the console. The engine makes a shrieking noise, coughs again, belching dark grey smoke in great plumes, and squeals to silence.

"Pile of fucking junk," he yells as a tall woman approaches through the smoke.

She laughs, wrinkled brown skin and dancing eyes, black hair scraped into a bun. So clear, and then gone, blurred into desert and sky. "So fix it."

"Fix it? On my wages? What am I, a fucking magician?" He's smiling as he speaks, swiping off his helmet to leap from the copter and salute her sloppily. "Millie. My lovely one. How's the desert treating you?"

"Like shit." She points at the copter, her finger elongating. An endless line. "Speaking of shit, you have scrap for me?"

Rubbing a hand stained with machine fluids over the stubble on his head, *into* his head, he says, "Be a waste to call it scrap. You could put this one to work salvaging. Body needs fixing a bit is all."

She looks sceptical. "You trying to squeeze more readies out of me, Hector Chen?"

"Millicent Bird, my lovely, have I ever?"

"Every. Damn. Time. Working out here doesn't affect my wits, you know."

He scoffs. "Your wits deserted you the second you thought the desert was a grand place to work. Missus Chen worries about you. News says the desert is growing in toxicity."

Millie laughs, loud and bright. The sound is a colour on the air. A streak of sun. "Tell the Missus to ignore the propaganda. It's bullshit. Desert ain't toxic, it's just bloody hot. Well, till night hits, then it's colder than Lilith's tits and throwing all manner of storms at you. Don't get me wrong, it ain't paradise by a *long* shot, but I got me some home comforts. An earth ship. A garden."

He shakes his head. Disbelief. "Grown with what? Water ration out here won't cover a garden!"

"Turns out even acid rain can be purified," she tells him. "What about you two? You know it ain't safe where you are. Never was. Where you planning to live when they come for your neighbourhood? Or when war comes to your city? Far as I can see, this is the only place left it's *safe* to try building a life. War stays far away, and you can't fucking gentrify a mountain of metal shit. All you can do is build it higher. This place will never change."

He makes a movement over his chest, a stab at something vaguely Catholic. "Never say never, lovely. Tempting fate, that."

"Superstitious twaddle, Hector. Think on it. I'll worry less if I know you're safe here, and we can fix this copter up for free then.

Deep Learning

What they don't know won't hurt 'em eh?" she says, patting his shoulder, the surface of it sticking to her hand, smearing through the air. "Now let's have a look at this salvager unit."

Millie climbs into the copter, wincing a little. Kneels in front of Niner, pulling a screwdriver from her breast pocket to poke at it. Its chest. Its limbs. The optics on its head unit. Niner tries not to flinch as the screwdriver elongates like fingers, glinting. Doesn't understand why that instinct occurs. It has no eyes to protect. Doesn't look remotely human any more to need to guard itself against uncanny valley response. And this is not artefact. The links are all but quiet; it has little sensory data interference, no artefacts except for those memories of Kitty, who was never linked. Whose shards are in a body that disintegrated into molten droplets of metal under the weight of fire. She's an artefact that should not exist. A glitch in its programming.

Millie hums. A pleased sound. Settles back on her heels to look out at Hector.

"You're not wrong about this one. It's in pretty good shape. I can fix it easy. Lucky me, I needed a new salvage unit now my knees are starting to act their age. And lucky you, your price just tripled."

He crows and rubs his hands together. "Protein for dinner tonight!"

Millicent Bird is a revelation.

In her care, Niner's current ancient body is re-hauled to work like new, the joints loosened and oiled, the solar cells that power it working at full efficiency. She discovers the secondary neural link, too, and though she cannot fix the mess made of it, she can add herself, and does so, making a few adjustments that allow her a two-way connection (*like* he *had, but* she *is not* he), figuring it'll make life easier to just think where she wants her newest Salvage unit to look today. Millie has an instinct about her mountains of scrap, and a dozen flying drones she sends out to look in likely locations first thing in the morning. All sailing off like birds, black dots against the skyline. A flock of bots.

In this way she knows the best place to look, knows exactly what's shifted to the surface in the heavy overnight storms, and which of

83

those parts she can sell for most remuneration.

Out in sun so bright and hot parts of its bodywork warp during the day, Niner *(feels?)* her in its links. Her mind is a perfect waveform built over the whispers of the rest. Brings no *(distress?)*. Her directives are *(soothing?)*. Spoken in Machine language, accompanied by coordinates so exact, Niner can wind precise routes through the vast panorama of metal mountains glinting in the sun and return to her warehouse, to her workstation in back, with the required salvage before the sun reaches its apex. Once it has all she wants, she sends it out to look for whatever it can find alone, always giving it a set location in which to dig, wary of the storms that come raging over the horizon as the sun sets.

Niner *(enjoys?)* these moments. In her usual unerring way, Millie seems to know where it can find parts of others like itself. Parts she can use to fix or improve it. To provide it with better joints. Better optics.

As it hunts, Niner begins to learn this unusual desert dweller it has ended up serving. This woman who can rebuild a broken robot in a junkyard in the desert so well it feels almost like it once was, though in truth it is nothing like it.

It learns first that she is younger than she seems. Only four and a half decades in age. That she was not always out here. Has only been here, in fact, for six years. Once upon a time, as all good stories begin (artefact), she was training to be like Dr Fischman, but war came to her city, a city far far away from here. That war spread like wildfire, and burnt everything she knew. Everyone. Like many citizens in those days, Millie took up arms herself. Tried to defend what remained. The army she joined, a ragtag, poorly armed band of guerrillas, managed to hold back the enemy for a year, and then were chased down and captured by one of those elite units, similar to the one still whispering piecemeal in Niner's net: seven out of twelve remaining.

She served eighteen years in a scrap yard just like this one.

Hard labour.

Those are the years that stripped the youth from her, left her this whip-thin husk, lined and weighed down. The years that made her knees old before their time.

They failed to steal her smile though. Her heart.

Niner is *(glad?)*.

It is changed since her hands have been inside its net. There is *(calm?)*. Niner is like blue wall. Blue sky. Endless. Serene. It is *(content?)* wandering the vast mountains of scrap, the sun following its progress through the sky, the clouds drifting past and through, bringing on their tails enormous angry storms that crash over the desert throughout the night. During those hours, before Millie sleeps, Niner and Millie sit in her earth ship, set into the side of a sandstone cliff and made with colourful bottles and pieces of scrap metal and plastic and listen to the howling wind by the warm crackle of a fire.

Millie sews.

Niner dismantles robot parts.

It is *(companionable?)*.

Niner designates the earth ship 'a house like her'. It could not make coherent what this means (not *name* not *attribution* but *absolute*), only that when it comes back to the house in the evening having outrun the storm, even if she is not there -- still in the warehouse at her workstation or out securing the solar sails and the antennae -- she is *there*. In every bottle, every scrap of metal rebuilt to a table or a window frame. In the greenhouse built along one side of the ship, curving around the edge of the cliff as it moves with the land. Amongst the tang of green things growing, the heavy weight of humidity.

And finding her *there* and *not there*, it will sit and wait for her return and feel that she is already present, and be filled with a quiet emptiness, a calm sense of purpose that need not be given form or action or expression.

That simply is.

In this way, almost without noting, weeks pass into months.

Months into years.

The mountains of scrap grow, swallowing yet more of the desert, of the view of sky and horizon. The days get hotter, the nights more violent. Storms tearing the desert apart, collapsing whole mountains of scrap, remaking the terrain. News comes of wars raging to the North, to the South-East, to the West. Of more famine, more flood, category four hurricanes in places there were none. Tornados. More tsunamis. Firestorms destroying crop domes. Volcanic activity. The violent shifting of tectonic plates. The world goes on, ever more at odds with itself. Failing and surviving by increments. Millie takes it all in with a jaundiced eye. Sometimes reaches to switch off the news with a decisive hand as if to say: enough.

Their visitors are few, but regular. The big copters fly over to dump new scrap at least once a day, usually around noon. They flash their lights as they pass, sometimes swooping low enough to wave, salute, or drop boxes of supplies too heavy for drones. Millie always makes sure Niner is nowhere near the intended drop site of metal or boxes, though she invariably asks it to carry the supply boxes in. Twice a month, military copters come to collect metal and parts. Private contractors come too: guerrilla groups, militia, the occasional nomadic caravan needing parts for repair. In this way, Millie eeks out enough to pay bills that never seem to end, despite the chaotic nature of the world, for those boxes of supplies, to send for a drone service delivering groceries or books or medication when she gets sick.

She rarely gets sick.

Three or four times a month, depending, Hector's little copter coughs its way over the peaks of the scrap mountains, bringing gossip, sometimes his wife's baking, and always larger scrap he's foraged himself from the military protecting the city, or from the city dumps. As the war and heat advance, he seems to grow more ragged. Thinner. Dark bags growing under his eyes. Grey prickling through the black stubble on his head. Millie worries about him, insists he take vegetables and fruit from her garden back to his wife, whole bags. Deprives herself to provide for them. She gathers intelligence about the war obsessively from every military unit coming from that direction, from the news, the patterns of warfare. Gives him warnings he never heeds. Repeats over and over the invitation to live here. To bring his wife and remaining family. To be safe.

Then a week comes around where Hector's copter doesn't appear on the horizon. Doesn't lurch its way through the mountains at all. Each day Millie goes out to watch, her lone figure a dark smear in heat haze and sunlight, rippling to complex puzzles of lines, and each day she is disappointed. One week becomes two. Then a month. Two months. Three. Four. Millie becomes frantic. She rejigs the radio to

Deep Learning

listen in to restricted military bandwidths. Illegal bandwidths. Tries to track what army may have reached the nearby city. What might be happening there. With no transport to take her, and no means of getting it, all she can do is listen and hope. It takes its toll.

She sleeps less, eats too little, becomes a too-thin sculpture of muscle, tendon and bone. Niner is *(afraid?)*. It is like she is disappearing. Niner tries to help. To be near. To be a *(comfort?)*, but she tells it to go. Go back to work. Stop hovering. It is then that Niner understands the difference between Niner and Hector. Niner keeps her company in the evening. Is *(companionable?)*, but is not *company*. Millie does not consider it *company*. This is logical. Niner is not real. It is not a person. It cannot be Hector.

But it is Millie's company.

A *(friend?)*.

And this realisation that she does not see it *(hurts?)*.

The cough of Hector's copter finally breaks the quiet of an afternoon almost fourteen months after his last visit, Millie drops her tools and tears out of the warehouse past Niner, midway through the deconstruction of a 4603 Unit it found the day before. Long since deactivated and more modern than its current body. It is *(thinking?)* of a refit. It turns to watch her go, the sun momentarily dazzling its optics, torqueing her tall, thin figure into a puzzle of colour smeared across the sand, a reminder of how it used to decode the world before the calm of her waveform filled its neural nets.

"Hey, Hector!" She waves madly as he lands. "Hey!"

Out there in the intense heat of the afternoon, they talk for a long while, two smears of heat haze and colour beside the vague shape of Hector's copter, before they melt into one another, a fierce hug, and Hector takes off again.

Millie walks back slowly, her shoulders slumped.

She taps Niner as she passes with the tip of a nail. "Work to be doing. Lots of work. Set to it."

"Hector returns?"

She stops. Shakes her head without turning around. "No. Hector's gone. He won't be back."

She continues to her workstation, where she stands for a moment and then lets out an almighty yell, a sound with shards of metal woven through it. Picking up a wrench, she throws it with all her strength, toppling a huge pile of crates, all filled with assorted parts. The sound it makes as it falls is deafening.

Over the rattle of parts escaping across the plastic flooring, Niner hears her say, "Fucking *bastards*! Fucking, *fucking*, bastards!"

Braced on her hands, Millie begins to sob. Awful, wrenching sounds.

Niner stands and watches. It is a friend, and it does not know what to do. Her link is turmoil. Is pain. The waveform turned to desert storm howling through mountains of steel. It has only command/respond language. She has never fixed that, because it is not broken but set and she has never seen the need to fix it. Never seen the need to communicate with Niner in any way but imperatives. Now it cannot tell her that it is sorry. That it will be okay. That Hector will be safe wherever he is gone.

It cannot tell her anything.

It can only stand, and witness.

Life continues, but is never the same.

Millie shrinks. Ages. Her thoughts through the link become hazy, shrouded in shadows. Their clarity fades into uncertainty as her body seems to wither away, that whip-thin silhouette of muscle, tendon and bone paring down until there is too much bone and too little else. Niner watches her eat, reaching for words that might make her eat more, understanding it both as the duty of care programmed in, and something less certain, something nebulous, attached to complicated thought patterns it cannot quite untangle but is nonetheless subject to.

It *(misses?)* how she was, how her waveform was like a light-beam played out from behind a cloud. Pure. Bright. Unmistakable. She is no longer recognisable. She is all shadows. It is like that sensory distortion has returned fully, but only for her essence in the link.

It would *(suffer?)* that old malfunction of its own senses to have her back.

Years tick past a day at a time. Slow, unchanging hours. The routine unassailable, with the exception of Hector's visits. Never again does his copter cough and lurch its way through the maze of precarious scrap mountains to shudder to a smoking halt outside Millie's warehouse. Never again does he salute. Or laugh. Or throw his hat into the cockpit. Or offer cooling packages of cakes cooked by Mrs Chen. His loss is more than the loss of Millie's clarity, her perfect waveform, it is like the holes left by those links that have died. There is *(grief?)* around this loss. As Millie weakens, Niner is required to take over more and more of her duties: arranging the drone flights as the storms die down with sunrise, marking out useful scrap, then not only collecting it but sorting it, dismantling it, pricing it. Hunting parts for its own body and replacing them.

In this time, the military copters dropping scrap begin to drop dozens of robots still partly functional. They are beyond good use, but it takes the time with each one to deactivate, taking out the neural nets.

These, it buries.

It should collect them, sell them on, but it finds itself *(unable?)*. These robots are just broken machines, mostly military and service units, they are not advanced models, they have no use, and yet it cannot allow that part of them, the *(mind?)* to go on for re-use. It is *(disrespectful?)*. They have served their time, fallen in battle or by overuse. Surely rest is their due? Millie has it take a drone cam out with it on its salvaging missions, so she can keep an eye on it, but it links itself directly so it can wipe these moments. More lies. Is this all Niner has learned from its links? It knows it lies well. But who will *(care?)* for the remains of these robots if Niner does not? When Niner cannot continue, it will have no Niner to bury its net, to ensure that it is not reused. Misused. So it does for these robots what will not be done for it. Because it must.

Millie dies quietly.

Her presence in its link simply vanishes, the hole of it far worse than the difference between the waveform and the haze. Out on the scrap mountains, Niner does not continue salvaging. It returns to her, to the earth ship, to bury her as it buries the nets of the robots it finds still activated. Her mind is gone, cannot be reused, and her body will rot, but it cannot leave her. That too would be *(disrespectful?)*. In the earth ship is a silence that is not the same as other silences. Profoundly empty. It did not realise how much presence a single life held until that moment. Does it have that presence? Or is its *(life?)* all pretence? All profound emptiness? It stands in the doorway, looking at her body in the chair, head dropped back, mouth slightly open. She looks peaceful, but there is no peace here. No calm. There is hollow. That flesh once held all of Millie, her thoughts, her laughs, her sadness, and now it is only meat.

Without Millie, the days continue much as they did with her.

Niner sends out the drones. Goes out to salvage the best of what the storms have unearthed. Sorts and dismantles. Finds robots and buries the nets of any it has to deactivate. The few visitors who come to purchase scrap notice no difference, long before she died Millie quit even that small role, choosing instead to sit on her rocking chair in the earth ship and sew, or read, or simply stare, her gaze too long, too distance. Too empty. Her gaze in its memory is always empty now. It only sees her eyes like glass, fixed and lifeless. It tried to close them before it buried her, but its hands were too large.

It ripped her eyelids.

It does not like to recall that. It tries to bury the memory as it buried her, but some things cannot be buried.

:::
:::
:::

Seven - Scrap

:::some things cannot be buried:::

:::

:::

:::

A memory surfaces that Niner does not want. A memory it is trying to conceal from itself. Trying to drown beneath a cascade of other memories. To delete. Overwrite.

That these things are long past. That it is remembering.

That it is buried.

:::

:::

:::

:::Niner is a dozen ghosts in a shell. A simulation. A game played out in the desert with the body and skills of a robot. Minds as game controllers. They think, it does, and the game becomes ever more bloody and violent by the second. As Niner is played, it learns, and as it learns and becomes ever more skilled at following their thoughts, their instincts, the game takes on ever greater complexity. They are already sending it into rescue missions like this, under heavy artillery, all alone.

Their number one asset they call it. Their secret weapon:::

:::

:::

:::

Much time has passed. This body fixed first by Millie and then maintained by its own hands, has long since rusted together.

It used to wait for winds to come.

91

Ren Warom

At night as the needles of light spearing in through gaps in the metal faded to darkness and its sensors picked up the roar of incoming storms, it would find itself paused, all processes suspended, waiting for that moment the storms might lift the weight on its body. But they did not. Somehow, the winds always passed over. Passed by. Collapsed mountains alongside, close enough to hear their metal tumble against the mountain on its body with a cacophonous roar, or too distant to hear anything, the collapses felt as vibration in the ground, translated upward by the shuddering of metals.

Now, even if this mountain were somehow next to fall, it could not save itself.

It is stuck here.

:::

:::

:::

:::its reaction to the noise in the silence is unexpected. (*Embarrassment?*) (*Shame?*) It (*wishes?*) for a moment to not be machine. Unreasonable. Humans in exo suits make these noises. It is not unusual. It is not limited to machine. This reaction is artefact. Unwanted. Not from the pain mind linked fresh and without warning, but from another. It cannot tell which. There are too many to sift:::

:::

:::

:::

A simple error in calculation brought it here. Errors robots cannot make. Niner should not have made such an error, categorically, except that day it was preoccupied with (*shards?*) (*slivers?*) (*shades?*) (*imprints?*) of Millie. It had gone to visit the grave it placed her remains into that morning, before it sent the drones out. Niner knew it (*missed?*) her company and could not process this artefact. Robots do not suffer for lack of company. Robots serve. And yet it was (*lonely?*) (*sad?*) (*grieving?*). Diverted. And forgot to check the delivery schedule.

Wrong place. Wrong time.

A simple error in calculation.

:::

:::

:::

:::time changes. Becomes a constant. The sun rising and setting a reliable metric. There are no more losses, no stuttering between being and doing, between self and selfless. No more black holes, though all those moments remain for it to examine, recorded into memory. (*Strange?*) to see from the outside what the thing they tried to make of it could and could not do. Mindless function struggling to obey imperatives in a battered body long past its usefulness. Memory is instructive. And (*painful?*):::

:::

:::

:::

When memory fails, the whispering links within its outer net are the only link it has to the living world. It suspends itself within them. They are faint now, the damage to its net rendering them nebulous. But there in the quiet, in the bright, boiling sun, if it is still and listens carefully, strains its sensors, it can reside within their lives. Those who remain. The unit, fighting this endless war. They have new members. Only three remain now of the dozen once linked to its net. All the rest are holes. Holes that were once lives. Whole people.

He is long since gone, too. *Marcus.* Assassinated.

Niner was there with him. Watching. The moment had less (*satisfaction?*) than it calculated. All it saw in his final moments was Kitty's face when he spoke to her on the phone. The desolation. The fear. His death did not change them. It could not. Kitty was gone, the shards of her lost in some scrap heap somewhere, in the remains of one of Niner's bodies.

Briggs moved far away. An outpost in the desert, servicing military units and exo suits. She married a specialist. Dr Speak, one of the women caring for the bodies inside those exo suits. Briggs had never settled in that new lab. Thought she'd never settle in the desert either, until she met Ruby. Now the desert seems beautiful. Or perhaps it is just Ruby.

Dr Fischman works alone. Still asks after Niner. But no one knows what she's talking about these days. They think she's starting to go senile. She knows it. Tries desperately to ignore it. It it deeply hurtful. Misses Decker dreadfully. He left the lab when Millie was still alive, years ago now, for a lucrative military contract in one of the last safe-house cities, taken when his partner became pregnant.

His daughter is twelve.

She builds robots.

Ren Warom

:::
:::
:::

:::flashes of activation under bright lights give Niner a disjointed view of itself. There is another body. It has been given another body. Thinner. Not combat ready. Refined. Sleek muscles and narrow hands and feet. There are suits on a rack. Expensive. Cuff links and a heavy watch whose value runs into the tens of thousands. Wing tip shoes, a whole row of them, placed just so on a shelf above the rack. The sensation of being rewritten, the usual phrases bringing unwanted compliance. The too-abrupt attachment of another mind. Too many faces. Broken howls. Blurred colours and darkness. Voices from the abyss:::

:::
:::
:::

Rain falls between the gaps, soft and relentless, dripping into its visual sensors. Before Niner joined Millie, years before, the rain was pure, free of the toxins that polluted rain in the cities. Scrap masters used to collect rain for everything, including drinking. But as the cities crept closer, swallowing the desert, the sky filled with their toxins. The rain was corrosive by the time Millie became scrap master. Is worse by far now, leaving rust and residue on the metals that gather into organic-looking blooms. These blooms grow on Niner, too. Eat away at its body, at its face shield. Given long enough, they will eat all the way through and into its net, swallowing everything that it is.

Before that, however, it will run out of power. It has over a dozen solar cells now, all salvaged from other units found on the scrap mountains, each capable of holding months of power, and it has been inert, using only enough to run memory.

But they will not last indefinitely.

Soon, it will sleep. And will not wake.

:::
:::

:::there is no panic. She does not scream. And as it reaches her, its greater weight allowing for propulsion, scooping her into its grasp, she doesn't struggle. She only wraps her arms around it and leans in, her breath serene:::

:::
:::

Eight - Specimen(?)

:::activate:::

Awareness steals darkness. Information flood occurs in simultaneous flow with data sorting, bringing the world into focus, briefly too bright and too loud, dialling down too swift to note the shock.

And Niner finds itself in a grey room, facing a large window.

The air is cool. Air conditioned. A brief hum in the background.

The lights are warm. Turned down low. They, too, hum.

The room is singing.

Beyond the window: lush green mountains. Not scrap: real. Rugged landscapes of trees, pocked grey and brown, a mixed palette, frosted white with mist at the tips. Below them, where their torsos dip gracefully to steppes and then to flatlands, spreads a large, still lake. Oval. A pool of melted silver. Of mercury. Trees range around it, their reflections swirling on its surface. Molten. Around them, above them, birds wheel in a low, grey sky, calling, calling, as the clouds roll on, roll in. There will be rain.

And Niner is… *(alive?) (reactivated?)*… for what purpose?

Seeking inside for guidelines, for expectations of service, Niner finds nothing. There are no imperatives. No protocols. No guidelines for service. There is only… a link. Singular and particular. A clear mind. Alert. *(Happy?)*. Like Millie's waveform this link sits bright and strong in its net, no distortions accompanying it, no warping of the world, no shadows.

Unlike the others, it is not imposed, it is offered.

Ren Warom

A gift.

"There you are. Awake at last. I knew you'd do it."

Footsteps tap across the cool white tile of the floor. Stop beside the window. Niner turns to look. It is a woman. *The* woman. The one in its drive. Her name is Gale. Dr Gale Thirsk. The lines of her face have a vague familiarity. It is like being haunted by a memory of Decker.

"You are Decker's descendent." It speaks without *(thinking?)* and is momentarily frozen, aware that it has spoken out of turn. It has...

"I am, his granddaughter in fact." She turns to lean her shoulder against the window, those eyes, all Decker's, regarding it with curiosity and a quiet sort of joy. She looks as if she has won something special. "Tell me how you're feeling, 5709. Are you fully functional?"

Niner was asked to confirm this status once before, a long time ago, at the very beginning, and had the means to answer stolen. Dr Decker, trying to fix it, built a bridge through the hurricane at the expense of expression. That bridge is gone. In its place is a full set of libraries, containing all languages. All words. All the words it might ever need. Waiting.

Where does it begin then?

There are no imperatives.

No protocols.

No guidelines.

But is not a question a guideline?

All Niner has to do is respond.

"I..." Is 'I' right? It does not feel wrong. It is not spoken in error, not programmed, but also not an artefact. Not this time. Niner begins again. "I would appreciate the designation Niner, if that is acceptable to you, Dr Thirsk, and I am... *well*. Where am I?"

She nods. "Niner. Got it. And if you're Niner, I'm Gale." Turning to indicate the view, Gale says, "As for where you are, the country is Vietnam, and this is the Fischman Lab, rebuilt brick by brick right here in Sapa, in the shadow of the mountains. The world is... changing. Rebuilding perhaps. Coming back from the worst, one hopes. This is one of a few places that survived, where we've come to begin again. Those of us who made it through."

Vietnam. Niner's knowledge of the world situates Vietnam far

96

from where it last was stationed. Where it was buried. "How am I here?"

She sighs. "Luck, and lots of hard work. We had so many teams out looking. My grandfather wanted to find you for Fischman, after she died, because of how she died, and where. She didn't deserve that, it was disrespectful. My mother took over the search when he retired, and I've been on her team for a decade. We found you seven months ago, in the Mid-American desert, what used to be the United States. The damage you'd suffered was extensive, and most of the team was afraid you might be inoperative." Gale turns back to look at Niner, a light in her eyes. "But I wasn't afraid, I've read all your data. You're like nothing I've ever seen, not even the E-cogs. Your patterns read human."

"I am not human."

She inclines her head. Acknowledgement more than agreement, as if it doesn't really matter. "Anyway, this is your room now. I thought you might enjoy the view. You can choose how to furnish it when you're ready."

"Gale, I do not require furnishings."

"But would you like some?" The question is off-hand, almost casual, and yet Niner senses through their link the challenge inherent within it, and feels an intense *(need?) (desire?) (interest?)* in rising to that challenge.

"I am... attached to the colour blue."

"Well then. That's a start. Do you know that, apart from perhaps the location, this is where you were born, Niner, within these walls." Touching Niner's arm, Gale offers a warm smile. "Welcome home," she says.

And there is, in that welcoming, an implicit permission, another challenge thrown. To change its designation. To take her gift and do with it whatever it wants. To be something worthy of a home. To be something worthy of furnishings.

To be *someone*.

To be Niner.

About the Author

Ren Warom is a writer of the weird and the speculative, variously published by Titan books, Apex Publications, and Fox Spirit Books. Currently Ren can be found questioning her sanity whilst juggling three spawn, eight cats, two books that won't shut the heck up, and one full time PhD. Life is invariably messy, but always interesting.

NewCon Press Novellas Set 7: Robot Dreams

What do robots dream of? Inspired by Fangorn's wonderful artwork, four of our finest science fiction authors determine to provide an answer in four stand-alone novellas.

Andrew Bannister introduces us to Kovac, an agent of the Mandate, assigned to a world whose inhabitants have no idea that they are an experiment. Kovac begins to realise there are agencies at work that have no place being there…

Ren Warom guides us through the lives of Niner, from soldier to body double to killer to scrap yard attendant. Niner only functions due to a malfunction that goes undetected, leaving its makers frustrated when they fail to duplicate their success.

Justina Robson shows us the rise of A.I., through subtle infiltration and more brazen manipulation, from gentle persuasion to blatant coercion, until the world is no longer ours. All for our own good, of course.

Tom Toner takes us to a primitive world where a bomb fell aeons ago, a world whose people will risk anything, even the monsters said to haunt the shores of Lake Oph, to mine the priceless substance known as *Gleam*…

www.newconpress.co.uk

IMMANION PRESS
Purveyors of Speculative Fiction

Breathe, My Shadow by Storm Constantine

A standalone Wraeththu Mythos novel. Seladris believes he carries a curse making him a danger to any who know him. Now a new job brings him to Ferelithia, the town known as the Pearl of Almagabra. But Ferelithia conceals a dark past, which is leaking into the present. In the strange old house, Inglefey, Seladris tries to deal with hauntings of his own and his new environment, until fate leads him to the cottage on the shore where the shaman Meladriel works his magic. Has Seladris been drawn to Ferelithia to help Meladriel repel a malevolent present or is he simply part of the evil that now threatens the town?
ISBN: 978-1-912815-06-7 £13.99, $17.99 pbk

The Lord of the Looking Glass by Fiona McGavin

The author has an extraordinary talent for taking genre tropes and turning them around into something completely new, playing deftly with topsy-turvy relationships between supernatural creatures and people of the real world. 'Post Garden Centre Blues' reveals an unusual relationship between taker and taken in a twist of the changeling myth. 'A Tale from the End of the World' takes the reader into her developing mythos of a post-apocalyptic world, which is bizarre, Gothic and steampunk all at once. Following in the tradition of exemplary short story writers like Tanith Lee and Liz Williams, Fiona has a vivid style of writing that brings intriguing new visions to fantasy, horror and science fiction. ISBN: 978-1-907737-99-2, £11.99, $17.50 pbk

The Heart of the Moon by Tanith Lee

Clirando, a celebrated warrior, believes herself to be cursed. Betrayed by people she trusted, she unleashes a vicious retaliation upon them and then lives in fear of fateful retribution for her act of cold-blooded vengeance. Set in a land resembling Ancient Greece, in this novella Tanith Lee explores the dark corners of the heart and soul within a vivid mythical adventure. The book also includes 'The Dry Season' another of her tales set in an imaginary ancient world of the Classical era.
ISBN: 978-1-912815-05-0 £10.99, $14.99 pbk

www.immanion-press.com
info@immanion-press.com